There was a world of difference between Moira Tennant, successful model, and Patrick Casey, famous playwright. But surely the feeling between them was strong enough to overcome their differences?

A WORLD OF DIFFERENCE

BY
SANDRA FIELD

MILLS & BOON LIMITED
15–16 BROOK'S MEWS
LONDON W1A 1DR

First published in Great Britain 1985
by Mills & Boon Limited

© Sandra Field 1985

Australian copyright 1985
Philippine copyright 1985
This edition 1985

ISBN 0 263 75061 2

Set in Monophoto Times 10 on 10½ pt.
01–0685 – 59389

Made and printed in Great Britain by
Richard Clay (The Chaucer Press) Ltd,
Bungay, Suffolk

CHAPTER ONE

MOIRA was bored. Bored, bored, *bored* . . .

She did not, of course, look bored. Far from it. She looked effortlessly, stunningly beautiful. As she wandered through the crowd, exchanging a remark or two here, helping herself to a canapé there, never really allowing herself to become involved, heads swivelled to follow her progress.

The women's eyes were generally calculating, their comments barbed.

'That dress must have cost a fortune. All those sequins and gold braid. And the pearls . . .'

'Darling, she gets all her clothes at a discount. After all, name one store in town that wouldn't want Moira Tennant wearing their spring collection. As for the pearls—well, look who she came with.'

There was indeed a man trailing in Moira Tennant's wake, like a portly tug following a sleek ocean-going yacht. While his tailor and his shirtmaker had done the best they could, the results were not encouraging considering the amount of money that must have been spent. His suspiciously dark brown hair was carefully combed to cover the maximum area of his scalp; he was perspiring.

'That's Anton Barber, isn't it?'

'One of the richest men in New York, my dear.'

Men's eyes also followed Moira Tennant's progress through the crowd, their expressions varying from the admiring to the frankly lustful. Moira noticed neither reaction. Admiration she had come to take for granted over the past four or five years, while lust she ignored. She stopped to chat with an ambassador and his elegant wife, introducing her escort; she rather liked Edwina Talcourt, who was confident enough of her own style

5

that she did not need to envy that of others. They discussed the Metropolitan Opera's production of *Don Carlo* and David Singer's sculptures at the Guggenheim; but although art galleries were one of Moira's escape mechanisms, the whole time they were talking the little refrain knocked against her skull: bored, bored, bored.

Some days she wondered if she would ever get rid of that refrain. It had built up insidiously over the winter, interposing what she thought of as a thick grey blanket between her and the people and activities she had once enjoyed. The blanket muffled the sound of music and voices, and dulled the colours of paintings and the sparkle of jewels. Worse, it dulled her own ambition and energy, which together with her unusual beauty had brought her to the pinnacle of her career as a model in the city where it mattered: New York.

With an actual effort of will Moira forced herself to concentrate on Trevor Talcourt's brilliant and amusing analysis of punk rock music. Anton, who was a fanatical devotee of Schoenberg and Hindemith, contributed a pungent comment or two: it was for these rare and often very funny asides that Moira continued to go out with him. In a casual way she was fond of Anton. His wealth meant nothing to her, something ninety per cent of the people in this room would not have believed. Anton, however, knew she was not interested in his money, and inwardly she was sure that was why he liked to go out with her—that, and the fact that she was a companion who added lustre to a man's reputation.

She helped herself to a glass of champagne from a silver tray offered by a uniformed waiter, and for a moment let her eyes wander around the room. The party was being given in the Park Avenue apartment of a television news commentator named Ted Price, who had his own highly successful weekly show; his tastes ran to contemporary abstract art, leather furniture, and, Moira had to admit, excellent champagne. She had done a widely broadcast interview with him three years ago, at about the time that her face was becoming known across the country in a cosmetics campaign. At that time Ted had wined and dined her, and had made a determined effort to get her into his bed. She had politely refused, he had accepted the rebuff in good grace, and they had been friends ever since. To be invited to one of his intimate Friday night parties was something of a cachet; that she should be bored here of all places was a very bad sign.

Absently she gazed at a ceiling-high oil that depicted a disconcerting tangle of faces not unlike the ones she used to draw as a little girl. Was bored the right word for the way she felt? Her mouth, exquisitely outlined in a golden-bronze lipstick, drooped unconsciously. Maybe depressed was a better word, she thought. Or miserable. Trapped. Lonely.

Ridiculous! an inner voice sneered. *What have you got to be unhappy about? You're one of the most beautiful women in New York, you've got lots of money, wardrobes full of clothes, a whole host of acquaintances. Unhappy? Nonsense!*

But, she cried back with a depth of anguish that took her by surprise, *there's not one person in this room who loves me. No one would really care if I walked out of the door and never came back. A few of these people like me, a great many of them envy me—but to none of them am I the most important person in the world.*

Well, whose fault is that? You've been so busy climbing to the top you haven't let anyone get close enough to love you. Have you? In fact, I wouldn't be surprised if you've lost the knack. Love is an art, you know. You have to keep in practice.

'Do I detect an all-absorbing interest in modern art?' a man's voice said into Moira's ear. 'You surprise me, Miss Tennant. I thought by definition all models were absorbed only in themselves.'

Moira came back to the present with a jolt. Turning her head, she encountered a pair of the bluest and most mocking eyes she had ever seen. They were also a good four inches above her own, and she was five feet nine in her stockinged feet. She said coldly, 'Who are you?'

He sketched a bow and said in a rich Irish brogue, 'Patrick Casey, at your service, ma'am.'

'The playwright.' The latest Patrick Casey production had taken Broadway by storm, and was still sold out several months in advance. Although she had seen the play, she had never met its author. It took only a split second to decide his newspaper photographs did not do him justice. Her preconception of a playwright was either of an effete young man waving a cigarette holder or of a paunchy, grey-haired debaucher of young women, who would wreath them in cigar smoke while busily undressing them. Patrick Casey fitted neither of those images. If she had been asked to supply one word to describe him, she would have unhesitatingly said 'tough'. Which was odd, because in a superbly fitting tuxedo he looked the epitome of the civilised man-about-town.

'None other.'

She had not forgotten his opening remarks. She said sweetly, 'Your plays are so original, Mr Casey, I would have thought you could have come up with a less hackneyed pseudonym. Or are you hoping to be mistaken for a far more famous Irish playwright?' She let her gaze wander over his thick black hair back to those incredibly blue eyes and added judiciously, 'You certainly have the good looks of a Celt. You should cultivate an air of melancholy, though—women, I am sure, would find that irresistible.'

'Whereas you find me quite resistible.'

'I am really not interested enough to make any kind of a judgment, Mr Casey.'

He said softly, 'First of all, Patrick Casey does happen to be my real name. Trite of me, I agree, but there you are. And secondly, why where you staring at that painting—with your mouth open, I might add—looking as if you'd lost your best friend, Moira Tennant?'

She looked around for someone to come to her rescue but the Talcourts had gathered two other couples into their circle and in the midst of it Anton was holding forth: no help there. 'I wasn't aware that we'd been introduced,' she said haughtily. 'How do you know my name?'

'How could I not recognise the most famous model in New York? Television, billboards, magazines—you're everywhere. *The enigmatic beauty, Moira Tennant, models Yves St Laurent's spring collection ... Miss Moira Tennant attends the wedding of the year ... Moira Tennant redefines the word blonde ...*' He peered at her hair with clinical interest. 'Does it come out of a bottle?'

If she had one vanity it was her hair, for it was thick and tawny, with a natural gloss and wave. She said gently, 'No more than yours does.'

'So the enigmatic beauty has claws. How does it feel to know that your face can sell anything from toothpaste to fur coats?'

'You haven't been following my career as closely as you would like to appear, Mr Casey, or you would know I never model fur coats.'

For a moment the mockery vanished, to be replaced by so intent an interest that she almost felt as if he had physically reached out and touched her. 'Really! Why not?'

'I happen to believe that the wild creatures of our world have enough pressures on them without me choosing to wear their pelts on my back.'

'Very admirable. On what other subjects do you have strong convictions, Miss Tennant?'

'I thoroughly dislike men who feel they have to attack me because of my profession. *I* have no problem with *your* profession, Mr Casey. So why should you have with mine?'

A waiter stepped between them. 'More champagne, madam? Sir?'

Deftly Patrick Casey put Moira's empty glass on the tray and gave her a full one. According to her preconception, a playwright's hands should be pale and attenuated. His were not. Tanned and well-kept, they looked very strong, as if they would be more at home with an axe than a typewriter. A shiver ran up her spine. Hastily she took a gulp of champagne.

He said debonairly, as if there had been no pause in the conversation, 'I suppose my difficulties arise because your profession, as you call it, is totally dedicated to the preservation of unreality.'

Her eyes glittered, and quite suddenly she realised she was no longer bored. 'So, surely, is yours?'

'Ah, no . . . through the admittedly artificial medium of actors and the theatre, I confront the audience with reality. In other words, the means I use are unreal, but not the end. Your job is artificial from beginning to end. It is obsessed with outward appearances, and says nothing about the person within.'

Somewhere deep within her his words struck a chord, and Moira knew with a strange kind of excitement that she had gained at least a partial clue to the stultifying sensations that had been overwhelming her lately. That, however, was no concern of his. She said shrewishly, 'How nice that you can justify your own job at the expense of someone else's.'

'Writing plays is hell on earth. I have to justify it somehow.'

'Then maybe we should both switch to something duller and more worthy—social work, perhaps?'

He laughed outright. Moira caught her breath. When she had first looked into those blue eyes she had decided he was easily the best-looking man she had ever seen—and in the course of her career she had seen a great many. He did not have the perfect features or the smooth profile of a professional male model, for his jawbone was far too determined, his nose was slightly hooked, and his eyes too deeply set. But when he laughed he had a vitality that was totally masculine—and to which she was forced to respond. Unwillingly she smiled back.

He said almost casually, 'The trouble is, you're utterly beautiful. I thought I was immune to that kind of thing. I spend a good part of my life tripping over beautiful actresses, after all. But right now I find myself with a strong urge to throw you over my shoulder and carry you out of the room.'

She fought back a blush—she, who never blushed. 'Uttering Tarzan-like whoops as you go?'

'Definitely. It would be good theatre, wouldn't it?'

'A most effective exit.' She took a sudden step backwards, alarmed by something in the blue eyes. 'Nevertheless, I would prefer you not to do it.'

'I must admit it's tempting. Quite apart from anything else, I'd like to see if I could disturb that admirable sang-froid of yours.'

'I think you would disturb more than mine. Ted's parties never descend to rowdiness.'

'As I tend to stay away from all parties, including his, I'm scarcely in a position to know.'

'Such an obvious cue,' she mocked. 'However, I shall oblige you. Why do you stay away from parties, Mr Casey?'

'The name is Patrick. Because they're a monumental bore.'

At his use of that particular word, Moira's eyes widened. They were magnificent eyes, tilted slightly at the corners, the irises a mysterious, changeable shade between grey and green; at the moment her lids were embellished with gold eyeshadow and her lashes with artfully applied mascara. 'A bore?' she faltered.

'A bore. You're bored, aren't you?'

'No! Of course not.'

'Come off it. I, along with every other man here, was watching you cross the room. You certainly looked bored to me.'

As she raised her chin the huge pearl drops at her earlobes swayed gently back and forth; they matched a twisted rope of pearls around her neck, bared by the wide neckline of her white jacket. There was nothing immodest about the jacket. It was encrusted with sequins and lavishly embroidered with gold braid, its sleeves long and tight, its bodice as snug-fitting as a vest. Yet it was obvious Moira wore nothing underneath it; and her long skirt of flowing white silk clung to her hips in sensual contrast to the stiffness of the jacket. She said without much conviction, 'I wasn't bored.'

'Bored out of your skull. The fact that every man within ten feet of you was longing to tear that very expensive outfit from your body obviously meant nothing whatsoever to you. Have you had so many men that you're no longer interested?'

Although she felt her nerves twang with annoyance, she allowed her lashes to brush her cheek demurely. 'So many that I've lost count,' she murmured.

He gripped her wrist with a strength that did not surprise her in the least. 'Is that true?' he said harshly.

Anger flared her nostrils. 'Do you honestly think I'd tell you—either way?'

'Oh, I'm sure it's true.' His fingers tightened their hold, although Moira would have sworn he was unaware of this action. With a primitive surge of her blood she knew that she would have to be in agony before she would beg for mercy from Patrick Casey.

From behind them their host said urbanely, 'It looks as though you two have already been introduced. That's good. When I spoke to you on the phone, Patrick, I said there'd be someone here I'd like you to meet—that someone is, of course, Moira,'

Not at all discomposed, Patrick Casey let go of her wrist, took a drink of his champagne, and said calmly, 'I don't think Miss Tennant is overly impressed with me.'

'I'm not sure that's so,' she responded, carefully refraining from rubbing her wrist. 'I once went to South America to photograph a collection of safari clothes, in the course of which I came face to face with a boa constrictor. I was very much impressed.'

Patrick gave a snort of laughter, and said kindly, 'Rather childish, Moira—but not bad.'

Ted was looking from one to the other of them, a sardonic twinkle in his eye. He looked like someone's kindly, middle-aged uncle, a pose which had caused more than one famous personality to reveal far more in front of the television camera than he or she had intended. He said, 'Maybe I should set up an interview with the two of you together.'

'No, thanks,' Moira retorted. 'Mr Casey doesn't approve of models.'

'All the better. An interview where everybody agrees with everybody else is usually boring.'

That word again. Moira said firmly, 'No interview, Ted,' and held out her hand. 'Thank you, it was a lovely party. But now I have to go home. I have an appointment at nine tomorrow morning, so I mustn't be late tonight.'

Ted kissed her on the cheek. 'Why don't you get Patrick to take you home? I don't think Anton's ready to leave yet.'

'I'm sure Mr Casey isn't at all interested in taking me home. I'll get a cab. Good night, Ted, and thanks again. Good night, Mr Casey.'

'On the contrary, I'm ready to leave now and I would be delighted to share a cab with you,' Patrick Casey interposed.

She said fretfully, 'We'll be the first ones to leave. *I* have to work tomorrow. I can't imagine the same applies to you.'

'Playwrights do occasionally work, Miss Tennant.' Patrick Casey gave the crowded room a leisurely survey. 'Although that's not my reason for leaving. With you gone, why would I stay?'

'Hardly a compliment to our host.'

Ted smiled amiably, said, 'I can stand it,' and wandered off in search of other prey.

Moira glowered at Patrick. 'I shall have to check with Anton.'

Anton was still talking to Trevor Talcourt, his Czechoslovakian accent more pronounced than usual, his tuxedo jacket unabashedly undone to reveal a tightly strained cummerbund. Quickly Moira explained the situation; she did not know whether to be glad or sorry when Anton waved an expansive hand and declared that he would much prefer to remain at the party provided she had an escort home. Although up until now Moira had always been glad that Anton did not have a jealous bone in his body, on this precise occasion she could have done with a display of possessiveness. Meekly she bent her head so he could kiss her on both cheeks, and bade farewell to the Talcourts.

The women's coats were in the guest bedroom, where a painting consisting entirely of neat parallel stripes in shades of red, yellow and orange stretched the length of one wall; the other wall was a vast mirror. Moira poked her tongue out at herself and pulled on her coat, a fine black wool lined with dark green silk. *You look gorgeous*, she told herself sarcastically. *And according to Patrick Casey, it's all fake.*

She stalked out into the hall, and in a frosty silence went down the private elevator with Patrick. The doorman was on duty. She waited in the foyer while Patrick hailed a cab, then dashed across the sidewalk, feeling the chill February wind bite into her cheeks. Giving the driver her address, she got in the cab and settled back in the seat, ostentatiously looking out of the window.

For some minutes they sat without talking. Then Patrick said flatly, 'I'd like to see you again.'

Startled, she looked round at him, her earrings bobbing. 'Whatever for?'

His laugh was less than amused. 'I have no idea. Just the same, I'd like to.'

The cab driver was weaving in and out of the traffic along the boulevard. Having no desire to lurch against her companion, Moira gripped the edge of the seat. 'You don't even like me,' she said.

In the flickering darkness his eyes had the intentness she had noticed earlier. 'I don't know whether I do or not. Maybe that's what I want to find out. But there's more to it than that. When I first saw you, you didn't just look bored—you looked actively unhappy. What were you thinking about, Moira?'

She drew her coat closer around her body and said in a brittle voice, 'It's obvious, isn't it? I was thinking about the total artificiality of my life.'

'Please—I really want to know.'

She felt as though she could hide nothing from those penetrating eyes, and somehow it did not seem right to evade him with another flip reply. 'Whether I'm happy or unhappy is nothing to do with you, Patrick,' she said slowly, unaware that she was using his name for the first time, knowing her words for the truth. She *was* unhappy. But there was nothing he could do about it. Nothing at all. 'I don't think we need to see each other again,' she went on. 'But do let me say how much I have enjoyed your plays. Particularly *Good Enemies*. I'm glad to have met you.' To the cabbie she added quickly, 'It's at the end of the cul-de-sac on the left,' and fumbled in her purse for her wallet.

'I'll look after the fare,' Patrick said roughly. 'And I'll see you to the door.'

She did not know him well, but she sensed there was no point in arguing with him when he used that tone of voice. She found her key and preceded him across the flagged walk into the little enclosure of brick town houses. They overlooked the churning, grey-green waters of the East River. Carried on the cold night air came the metallic clang of traffic from the Queensborough Bridge.

Hers was the second house in. It had a tiny garden with a magnolia tree and a patch of grass surrounded by wrought iron railings; her front door, window frames, and shutters were painted navy blue, in daylight an attractive contrast to the mellow pink brick. The fittings were brass.

Moira unlocked both bolts and stepped inside, turning to face Patrick. 'Thank you for bringing me home,' she said formally.

He was standing on the step below her, his face level with hers. He said quietly, 'I have the feeling we'll meet again. I hope so. Good night.' Wheeling, he ran down the steps, and she heard the click of his heels on the path, then the slam of the cab door. Quickly she closed her own door, slipping the bolts in place and sliding the chain into its slot. Flicking on the lights, she walked into the kitchen and poured herself a glass of milk.

Her house was the smallest of the ones in the row that faced the river; downstairs she had a kitchen, living room and tiny dining alcove, and upstairs two bedrooms and a bathroom. She had bought it from a business acquaintance two years ago, horrified by the horrendous price yet knowing it could not fail to be a good investment, nor had she ever regretted its purchase. It was the one place in this immense city where she could be alone. And it was hers. Perhaps in reaction to the awesome complexity and ruthlessness of the city she had decorated the apartment in warm muted shades; the few paintings were tranquil and well-drawn; the carpets soft and the furniture comfortable. She allowed herself the indulgence of flowers all winter, and almost always had music playing somewhere in the house. And finally, she rarely allowed her cherished privacy to be shared. Once or twice a year she gave a party, and occasionally she might invite a woman friend for lunch or dinner; but almost never a man. She had long ago decided there were enough restaurants in New York that she did not need to do that, although she had never analysed the reasons behind her decision.

Glass in hand, she went through to the living room, flipping on a light and sinking into the velvet-covered chesterfield. The scent from a pot of narcissus on the cherrywood coffee table drifted to her nostrils, and idly she admired the waxen gold-centred petals. Now that she was alone she could admit to herself that she had been tempted to accept Patrick Casey's invitation. He was like a dormant volcano, she thought fancifully. Outwardly normal, inwardly seething with life. Certainly in their brief encounter he had succeeded in arousing emotions in her that had long been dormant. It was just as well she had refused to see him again. She had problems enough right now without adding a personality as forceful as his to her life. And, contrary to what he had said, it was highly unlikely that they would meet again . . .

CHAPTER TWO

THE February days passed one by one, blustering and foul-tempered. On the streets pedestrians hunched into their clothing against the biting wind, their faces as grim as the weather as they dodged the puddles and the heaped-up dirty slush. Traffic jams snarled at every corner. In Central Park the trees lifted their bare, tangled limbs to the leaden skies; the grass was dun-coloured, the rocks rimed with ice.

Moira heard nothing more from Patrick Casey. Her private telephone number was unlisted, but she knew he could have obtained it from Ted had he wanted to; she could only conclude he had not thought it worth the effort. She should have been pleased. She was not.

Her workload was extremely heavy. Once a year she did an intensive three weeks of studio sessions and public appearances for her exclusive cosmetics contract. The three weeks were wearing, but the pay was extremely good; up until now she had in no way begrudged the time, being astute enough to know that jobs like this enabled her to own the little town house by the river. However, this year was different. She was far too much of a professional to let her personal feelings affect her performance, but by the end of each day her nerves were at screaming point. She was tired of spending hours in front of a mirror, tired of having the exact angle of her head or the precise shade of lip gloss considered as a matter of earth-shaking importance. What did it matter if she wore honey-gold or dusty apricot? Patrick Casey would certainly not consider it relevant.

It took energy and a rigorous effort of will to keep these thoughts to herself. By the time the three weeks were up and she had returned from a whirlwind five-day tour of resort hotels in southern California, Moira was exhausted. The sun had shone each day she was there, and even though the cosmetic company's art director had made it very clear she must not get a tan, her frayed spirit had revelled in the clear blue skies, the gently waving palms trees, the gloriously hued blossoms, To come back to the grime and sleet of New York was a horrible anticlimax. The cocooned comfort of her little house seemed claustrophobic rather than attractive; she should be lying on a Californian beach rather than turning up the thermostat and having a hot bath to take the chill from her body. Swathed in a long velvet robe, she plunked herself down on the chesterfield to watch a television play.

It was not a very good play. In fact, it was a very bad play. Patrick Casey could have improved it, Moira thought, scowling at the screen. He would probably have scratched the whole thing and started over again. Or maybe he wouldn't have bothered.

The telephone rang. She picked up the receiver and said grumpily, 'Hello?'

'It's Margarita. Where have you been? I've been trying to get you for three days.'

Moira grinned, her spirits lifting. Margarita Stendal was a senior executive in an advertising agency. A chic, intelligent thirty-year-old divorcee, she somehow packed into each twenty-four hour day a career, single-parenting, and an active social life. Moira was one of the few people who knew that Margarita's deepest commitment was to her daughter Shelley: the advertising agency never guessed it.

'Just back from San Diego,' Moira said airily.

'Lucky you! Couldn't you wangle a two-month extension?'

'I wondered why I hadn't the minute I stepped off the plane in New York—isn't the weather foul? How's Shelley?'

They exchanged the latest news, then Margarita said, 'I don't suppose you're free tomorrow night? I've had two tickets for Patrick Casey's new play for months, I invited this absolutely gorgeous ad-man, and yesterday he had his appendix out. So no date. I'm sorry for him but I'm sorrier for me.'

'You must have lots of other men you could invite.'

'I'd rather go with you. We haven't had a get-together for ages.'

Moira hesitated, then said slowly, 'I saw the play a few days after it opened in the fall. But three or four weeks ago I met Patrick Casey. I'd love to see it again now that I know a little bit about him.'

'You *met* Patrick Casey? How did you manage that? They say he's a bit of a recluse. Spends half his time in the wilds of Canada and the rest being unavailable for comment.'

'It was at a party.' Moira added reluctantly, 'He didn't like me very much. Thought I was bored and artificial.' She did not add that he had also thought she was unhappy.

'Then his taste is atrocious,' Margarita said stoutly. 'The play starts at eight. Why don't we meet at the theatre, and then we could have a snack afterwards. I've discovered this marvellous little Greek restaurant, their baklava is out of this world. I'll reserve a table, how about it?'

Margarita always knew of a marvellous little restaurant somewhere. 'Sounds wonderful. I'll look forward to it.'

'See you tomorrow then. Bye, Moira.'

Moira put the phone down. On the television screen her own face was looking out at her, adjuring the viewers to buy a particular brand of shampoo. She looked at herself critically, deciding the cameraman had done a good job in capturing the highlights in her hair. The lipstick was a touch too glossy, though. She must remember that next time.

Just as the commercial switched to a hairy-chested man bouncing a shiny red truck over a great many rocks, the telephone rang again. This time it was Peter

Hazelton, the art director for a top fashion magazine. He too had been trying to reach her for the past three days, and again she explained where she had been. Peter, as usual, was in a hurry, and continued speaking almost before she had finished.

'I've got an assignment lined up for next week. Probably two full days. Derek Nash is the photographer. We want to do an article on Patrick Casey while he's in town. The idea is to call it "A Man For All Seasons", and have a four-page spread, you and he together in outfits for spring, summer, fall, and winter. Then one of our feature editors will interview him. How about it?'

She took a deep breath. 'Does he know about this?'

'Well, of course. We had to approach him first. Good publicity for him—not that he needs it.'

'Does he know it's with me?'

'No. We don't know that ourselves yet, do we? Yes or no, Moira?'

She liked Peter, even though he sometimes irritated her unbearably. 'Hold on while I get my appointment book.'

The book was upstairs in her bedroom. As she ran up and down the staircase, she thought of spending two full days in Patrick's company, and knew exactly what she was going to tell Peter. Nevertheless, she turned the pages of her leather-bound book to the following week, and said in a neutral voice into the receiver, 'Thursday and Friday are free.'

'Good. Nine o'clock on Thursday at Derek's studio. You know where it is, don't you? 18th Street.'

'Yes,' she said drily. 'You'd better warn Mr Casey that it's me—he doesn't like models.'

'We'll treat him with kid gloves, darling. See you then.'

Smiling a little lopsidedly, Moira replaced the receiver. Peter never wasted time on social graces like saying hello or goodbye. Peter never wasted time at all. Although at the age of twenty-seven he excelled in a highly responsible position, her private concern was that he would burn himself out by the time he was forty.

She had totally lost interest in the play by now, so she switched off the television and picked up a book. But as she was reading and then getting ready for bed, she was aware of a quiver of anticipation at the back of her mind. Next week she would see Patrick Casey again. His prediction would come true.

The marvellous little Greek restaurant was all that Margarita had promised. The decor was attractive without being pretentious and the menu was varied. As a sop to her conscience Moira ordered a salad, then ruined her good intentions by following it with baklava. 'I shouldn't,' she sighed. 'I put on three pounds the week I was in California.'

'You can afford it,' Margarita said unsympathetically, for she had a tendency to put on weight very easily. All on her hips, as she laughingly complained. She had a narrow, intelligent face with good bones, dark brown eyes, and a cap of shining auburn hair which was never as tidy as her hairdresser intended, for Margarita had a habit of running her fingers through it. Pondering the wine list, she asked, 'What did you think of the play, seeing it for the second time?'

Moira was still under its spell. 'It impressed me just as deeply this time as last. He has a wonderful comic touch, hasn't he? Remember the scene at the end of the second act when they're all talking at once? That was so *funny* ... and then in a line or two he brought all Samuel's anger to the fore.'

'And Sara ... I cried buckets over Sara.'

'So did I.' Moira frowned. 'The anger was very real, as was the despair, because you knew she was going to die. Yet somehow the overall message was one of compassion and of hope. Don't ask me how he did that.'

'If we knew, maybe we'd be famous Broadway playwrights! You said you met him, Moira. He must be a man of tremendous depth and insight.'

Moira wrinkled her nose. 'When he turns his full attention on you, you feel like a beetle on the end of a pin. You can wriggle all you like, but you can't get away.'

'You mentioned he didn't like you?'

'I don't think he did. He thought my whole lifestyle was fake and artificial.'

'Bit of a nerve for a complete stranger to categorise you like that.'

'Exactly what I thought—and said.'

'*Are* you happy with your lifestyle, though, Moira?' Margarita asked gently. 'The last two or three times I've seen you, I've thought you looked a bit—lost.'

Ridiculously, Moira felt like crying; maybe it was a delayed reaction to the play. 'I don't know what's wrong with me!' she burst out. 'Everything's fine—I'm at the top of my field, I've got lots of money and a nice house. I've worked for years to get where I am now. Yet now that I'm there, none of it seems to mean very much. I feel as if I'm going through the motions.'

'On automatic pilot, as it were.'

'Yes. But when you put a plane on automatic pilot it's so you can do other things. I'm not doing anything else—I'm just existing.' Her voice wobbled. 'And I can't talk to anyone about it, they'd think I was going crazy. You're the only one I've said anything to.'

The waitress brought them hors d'oeuvres of pâté and feta cheese. When she had gone, Margarita said thoughtfully, 'You're not going crazy. But I think your body's trying to tell you something, and maybe you'd better pay attention. You've worked terrifically hard for years, Moira. How many years exactly?'

'Nearly eight. I was eighteen when I first came to New York.'

'So in about five years you went from a complete unknown to one of the top models in the country. That didn't just happen. You worked at it.'

'I sure did.' Moira could remember herself at eighteen as clearly as if it were yesterday. She had been Maura

MacLeod then. She had come from a little coal-mining town in Cape Breton, and New York had terrified, exhilarated, baffled and confused her. With the brashness of ignorance she had gone to the top modelling agency in the city; it had been the most exciting moment of her life when she was told she had potential. She had gone from photographer to photographer building up a portfolio; she had learned about make-up and grooming and had cultivated a veneer of sophistication; she had been put on the books in the agency; she had eventually been sent to Europe to expand her portfolio and cultivate her innate sense of style. She had worked. Oh God, how she had worked! Hours of lining up for auditions. Days in the studio being photographed for catalogues, until her legs ached and her back hurt and her eyes burned . . . Oh yes, she had worked.

'I've known you for five years, so I can remember you in those days,' Margarita persisted. 'Your whole life revolved around getting to the top. It used to frighten me sometimes, you were so single-minded about it. You wouldn't go to parties because you might get circles under your eyes. You dieted and exercised to keep a twenty-three inch waist. You ate all the right foods and didn't dare get a tan. You weren't just working as a model from nine to five. You *were* a model—twenty-four hours a day.'

'But it paid off,' Moira said defensively. 'I made it to the top, didn't I? First I broke into television and then I got the cosmetics contract. After that I had it made.'

'Yes, you made it to the top. I'm sorry if this sounds like a cliché but it's the only way I know how to put it. Somewhere along the way, you became Moira the model and you lost Moira the woman.'

Moira shifted uncomfortably. 'That's not true.'

'I believe it is. How long since you've been in love, Moira?'

'A woman doesn't have to have a lover to be complete.'

'We all need love ... How long since you've had a real holiday?'

'I've just come back from California.'

'A holiday, I said.'

'Every time I go away, I miss out on a good contract—it never fails. So I guess I've got out of the habit of taking holidays.'

'I guess you have.' Their plates were taken away, and a salad of greens and fish, redolent with garlic, was put between them. 'I'm going to be very directive, and then I'll shut up and mind my own business. I think you should take at least a month off, Moira. Maybe even two. Get right out of the city. Go somewhere you've never been before, go home, go wherever you like. But go. And if you can have a rip-roaring affair while you're gone, all the better.' Margarita gave her a comical grimace. 'Please pass the bread and don't hit me with the wine bottle. I don't usually go ladling out advice like this, do I?'

Obediently Moira held out the wicker basket of hot crusty bread. 'If I went away, I'd miss the——'

'That's the choice you have to make,' Margarita interrupted, running her fingers through her hair. 'Which is more important—your career or yourself?'

'You're being very forceful.'

'I'm feeling very forceful.' Abruptly Margarita rested her hand on Moira's. 'We've been friends for a long time. I care about you. And please don't get me wrong—I admire and respect you for all you've accomplished. But the cost is starting to catch up with you. I'm convinced it's time you got away and took a long hard look at the future.' She gave Moira's fingers a little squeeze. 'And now I really will get off my soapbox. Isn't this bread scrumptious?'

'Mmm.' At random Moira heard herself say, 'I'm doing two days of fashion shots with Patrick Casey next week.'

'Two *days* ... with Patrick *Casey*! Oh, you lucky thing! I'd give my eyeteeth for half an hour with that man.' Margarita's brown eyes narrowed with calcula-tion. 'Now there's a candidate for your affair. Why don't you work on him?'

'Nonsense! This is purely a business arrangement.'

'It doesn't have to stay that way.'

'You said you'd get off the soapbox.'

'So I did ... but you will think over what I said, won't you?'

'Promise.' Moira smiled at her. 'And thanks—you're a good friend. Now why don't you tell me about this ad-man?'

'Six feet tall, hair as red as mine and a temper to match. I visited him in hospital this afternoon on my way home from work. I must admit he seemed pleased to see me.'

'I should hope so. Any man would be ... Do you ever think of remarrying, Margarita?'

'Sometimes. Although it scares me to death, because I couldn't stand to go through a second divorce. So my standards are pretty high. Too high, I expect. It would certainly be better for Shelley to have a stepfather rather than a succession of "Mommy's friends".'

'Hardly a succession. You've only had one serious relationship since your divorce.'

'And that didn't work out.' Margarita poked at her lettuce. 'That's one thing I can never understand about you, Moira—you don't seem to need men. Oh, I know you go out a fair bit, you're seen in the right places at the right times. But you're not emotionally involved, are you? I always seem to be madly attracted to somebody or other. Which at my age isn't particularly suitable.'

'You're thirty, not sixty!'

'Some days thirty feels like sixty ... Yummy bread, isn't it? Shelley's latest craze is that I should stay home and learn how to make bread. Can you visualise me doing that?'

'Wearing a cute little apron!' They both laughed, and to Moira's relief the talk moved to other, less

contentious matters. The baklava, which was dripping
with honey, was consumed with considerable pleasure,
and by midnight Moira was home. Normally she was
delighted to close the door behind her and relish the
peace and silence of her house. But tonight, perhaps
because of the conversation with Margarita, she found
herself wondering what it would be like to have
someone waiting for her with whom to share the events
of the day. Someone who loved her. Someone who
would follow her upstairs to the bedroom and make
love to her ... she shivered, for in her mind's eye she
saw Patrick Casey's blue eyes burning into hers, and felt
his fingers on her wrist. Someone like Patrick Casey ...

CHAPTER THREE

ON Thursday morning Moira took a cab to 18th Street, where Derek Nash had his studio on the top floor of what had once been an office building. He had stripped the single large room to its hardwood floor and bare white walls, installed a bathroom, a make-up area, and a cupboard for equipment, His sole concessions to comfort were three or four wooden chairs and a kettle to make coffee. He was an austere young man with gold-rimmed glasses and tight black curls, every bit as ambitious as the Moira of eight years ago, and just as professional. Although Moira respected him, she did not particularly like him, for he had no sense of humour whatsoever, taking himself as seriously as his work.

She arrived at the studio at two minutes to nine, running up the narrow wooden stairs and ringing the bell. Derek unlatched the various locks and bolts; he was convinced the underworld had an acquisitive eye on his camera equipment and was only waiting for him to slip up on his security to seize every last filter and roll of film. 'Good morning, Moira,' he said, checking his digital watch. 'Right on time. Mr Casey has been here for ten minutes.'

'Then he was early, wasn't he?' she said pertly, giving Derek a dazzling smile. He smiled back, looking as if his face muscles hurt. She added, 'Is everyone else here?'

'Peter and Sharon are. Gwendolyn should be along any minute.' Gwendolyn was the stylist, responsible for whatever garments the models wore.

Moira walked into the studio, as always admiring the proportions and sense of space. As she had expected, Patrick Casey was standing by one of the windows. 'Good morning, Mr Casey,' she purred. 'You said we would meet again.'

28

'So I did.'

He was taller than she remembered and altogether more formidable in dark cords and a sheepskin jacket. The man of the axe rather than the typewriter. He did not look overjoyed to see her, she decided, swinging her loden green cape from her shoulders and putting it on the back of one of the chairs. Her designer jeans, tucked into leather boots, were skin-tight.

He was regarding her quizzically. 'So this is how you look in your natural state.'

Her face was scrubbed clean and her hair hanging straight down to her shoulders. Suppressing the impulse to say something thoroughly vulgar, Moira remarked limpidly, 'The real me. Take it or leave it.'

'That's far too difficult a decision this early in the morning.'

'You do look a little hung over.'

'I am. A very tedious party last night with too many aspiring actresses hanging on to my every word and telling me how wonderful I am.'

'Nice for you.'

'Boring. I missed you.' She raised her eyebrows in polite disbelief. 'I missed you the past few weeks, too, I was away on a publicity tour.'

Was that why he hadn't been in touch with her? 'I was away, too,' she said coolly. The unspoken message was clear: *I wasn't sitting home waiting for you to call.*

With the sensual grace she had learned many years ago she walked across the room to the make-up cubicle. Sharon, a frizzy-haired blonde, was laying out her array of brushes and creams on the counter, while Peter, red-haired and as highly charged as an electric coil, was sorting through the array of garments on the metal rack.

'Morning, Moira,' he announced. 'Anytime you're ready Sharon can start on you. We're going to do the spring shots first.'

Rain was rattling against the grimy windowpanes. 'Good idea,' Moira said wryly, perching herself on a stool.

'Make her look about nineteen, Sharon, sweet, demure, as if butter wouldn't melt in her mouth. Ingenue stuff, got it?' He threw a xeroxed sheet on the counter. 'Hair piled up, lots of curls and tendrils. Daisies stuck here and there. Gwendolyn's supposed to bring the flowers, where the hell is she?'

'She's always late,' Moira said easily. 'Relax, Peter.' Which was useless advice, she knew.

By the time Sharon had wound Moira's hair in heated rollers, skewering them with metal pins, Gwendolyn has rushed in, her arms full of daffodils, her Boston twang deploring the New York subway system and the iniquities of cab drivers. She was a widow of fifty-odd with a seamed face and a tough manner that hid a heart as romantically inclined as a teenager's. While her own clothes always looked as if they had been grabbed from the closet by someone who was blindfolded, her taste for the models was unerring, and Moira always enjoyed working with her.

Sharon set to work on Moira's face. She had brushed on under-eye cover and foundation and had outlined Moira's mouth with a lipliner pencil when Patrick sauntered in. He blinked at the sight of her. Irrepressibly Moira winked at him in the mirror. 'Hold still,' Sharon said severely, following the line of Moira's lids with a pencil.

Demanded Patrick, 'How long will this take?'

'Fifty-five minutes for Moira,' Sharon replied crisply. 'Fifteen minutes for you.'

'Because you're nearly perfect as you are,' Moira murmured.

The look he gave her was enough to curl her hair without benefit of rollers. Turning on his heel, he strode back into the studio. Gwendolyn rolled her eyes heavenward. 'What a hunk! If I were twenty years younger . . .' Moira noticeably made no reply.

It was nearly ten-thirty by the time they were ready to start shooting. Moira looked delightful in a tea gown of white cotton and lace with a great many flounces and ruffles, its square neckline delicately hinting at the swell of her breasts, its full skirt falling to her ankles. Her lip gloss was pale pink, her eyeshadow a wistful green. Patrick, arrayed in a very becoming beige linen suit with a striped shirt, looked thoroughly out of sorts. Ignoring this, Peter began organising them. Against a backdrop of blue sky and fluffy white clouds, Moira was perched on a stool with Patrick standing at her side offering her a large bunch of daffodils at which she was to gaze demurely. Peter fussed around them, rearranging the daffodils, tweaking at Moira's dress, and adjusting the set of Patrick's jacket. Finally satisfied, he backed off.

The studio lights glared down on the little tableau. Derek ordered, 'Move a little closer to her, Patrick.'

As Patrick obeyed, Moira felt the hardness of his body against her shoulder and felt his breathing stir the tendrils of hair that coiled artistically down her neck. She stared into the ingenuous yellow faces of the daffodils, knowing her heart was beating erratically, cursing herself for being so unprofessional. She'd worked with dozens of male models—why should Patrick Casey be any different from the rest?

In a deadpan voice Derek said, 'Okay. It's springtime. Birds are singing, and grass is green, all's well with the world. You've fallen in love with this beautiful creature in the white dress, Patrick, and she's just accepted your bouquet of flowers. You're happy, she's happy, the whole world's happy. Let's get started. I'll run through a couple of polaroids first.'

Moira stifled a giggle and gazed soulfully at the daffodils. The flash went, she altered the angle of her head and it flared again. 'Relax while I check these out,' Derek suggested.

As he and Peter held a low-voiced conference behind the camera, Patrick straightened, muttering for Moira's benefit alone, 'The world of illusion. You do look about nineteen. What's even more unbelievable is that you look virginal. Well done, Moira Tennant.'

She had never known anyone who could irritate her

as easily as he. 'It's my job to look the way they want me to look!' she snapped, her lace-covered bosom heaving.

From behind the camera Peter tugged at his red curls and exclaimed, 'You're in *love*, you two! Quit glaring at each other. Patrick, I don't care if you hate her guts in real life. Right now you're wooing her, you adore her, she's the answer to all your dreams. We'll do a roll in the same pose, then we'll change positions. Ready? Let's go.'

'How many on a roll?' Patrick demanded in an undertone.

'Thirty-six,' she whispered back.

'And that's just a *start*?'

'He'll take two or three hundred shots altogether this morning.'

'Good God. I thought it would be a matter of him taking one or two photographs and then we'd go home.'

'Are you two quite ready?' Derek said acerbically.

'No,' said Patrick. 'Are we going to be standing around like this for the next *hour*?'

'That's right.' Derek adjusted the focus.

'You mean I've got to act as if I'm in love with her for a whole hour?'

'Right.'

'And keep holding on to these bloody daffodils?'

'You got it.'

Moira had had enough. She turned her body and glared up into Patrick's face. 'You're involved in the theatre,' she fumed. 'You must know something about acting. Look upon this as a challenge. You've got to convince the world you're prostrate at my feet—surely the wonderful Patrick Casey can do something as simple as that?' With consummate artistry she allowed her body to sway towards him, her eyes to grow luminous, and her mouth to soften. 'Come on, Patrick,' she cooed. 'I'm your heart's desire.'

In his eyes she saw fury struggle with laughter; then something else sparked in the blue depths, an emotion that made her breath catch in her throat. His face was coming closer. Her blood began to race in her veins.

As the flash exploded, the shock rippled through her body. But Patrick's expression did not change. *He's acting*, she thought frantically. *He's doing exactly as you suggested.* She called on every ounce of her professionalism, changed the angle of her chin and smiled sweetly into his face.

'Keep it up,' Derek said, with the nearest thing he allowed himself to excitement in his voice. 'Great shots.'

And keep it up she did. That was what she was being paid for, wasn't it? At the end of the roll, Michael had them both stand, the flowers in the crook of Moira's elbow, Patrick's arms around her waist. Another roll was shot. Then they walked towards the camera, her eyes downcast, his body hovering over her with all a young man's ardour.

It seemed to go on for a very long time. When Derek finally pronounced, 'Okay. That'll do. Meet here at one-thirty for the winter shots,' Moira was exhausted. It was no help that Patrick removed his arm from her waist and stepped away from her as fast as he could, the softness vanishing from his face as if a switch had been turned off. Giving her a curt nod he disappeared into the bathroom to change. Minutes later, from the make-up cubicle, she heard him call to Derek, 'I'll be back at one-thirty,' and then heard the door click shut behind him. For some reason she had pictured the two of them enjoying a cosy lunch together ... how wrong she had been. He couldn't wait to see the last of her.

Her shoulders sagged as Gwendolyn patiently unfastened the row of tiny, covered buttons down her back and eased her arms out of the dress. 'You looked darling,' Gwendolyn confided. 'Just darling. Maybe it'll turn into a real-life romance. You make such a handsome couple—he's so tall and dashing.' She sighed, shaking out the lacy folds of the dress. 'Most of the women in New York would have given a million dollars to be in your shoes this morning.'

Said shoes, white satin pumps with little bows on them, had been pinching Moira's feet for the last hour. She said flatly, 'Mr Patrick Casey cannot stand the sight of me, and I'm sure he'll be delighted when this is over.' Gwendolyn looked so crushed that Moira added hastily, 'Let's go for lunch together, Gwen—isn't there a little Italian place just around the block?'

'Yeah ... but you did look lovely together.'

Sure. Lovely. If the man ever gets tired of writing plays, he can make a fortune acting in them, Moira thought sourly, hauling on her jeans with unnecessary vigour.

A delicately flavoured lasagne and a long discussion of Gwendolyn's gentleman friend, who apparently was wildly romantic under a rather placid-looking exterior, served to improve Moira's mood. When they got back to the studio, a security van was parked outside. 'That's for the rubies,' said Gwendolyn. 'You're going to knock his eyes out this afternoon.'

She certainly represented a vastly different person from the shy young girl with the daffodils, Moira decided an hour-and-a-half later as she surveyed herself in the cubicle's full-length mirror. Her hair had been pulled back into a severe knot on the back of her head, her eyeshadow was a provocative blending of charcoal and burgundy, her lipstick the same rich burgundy. Her evening gown was unrelieved black, slit from the floor to mid-thigh, worn with gossamer-sheer black stockings and black sandals with excruciatingly high heels. Over the whole outfit she wore a floor-length cape of shot taffeta in a rich wine-red, a massive ruby and a diamond brooch fastening the high collar, matching earrings hanging at her lobes. A single square-cut ruby glowed on one finger. The security guard lounged on one of the wooden chairs, watching her every move.

She walked through the narrow doorway of the make-up cubicle into the studio, where Patrick was waiting for her. Over a tuxedo and a pleated white shirt, he too was wearing a cape, his thigh-length, fashioned of supple black leather. He looked magnificent, she thought helplessly, a virile male animal under a thin veneer of civilisation. If he were to seize her now and carry her out of the room over his shoulder, what would she say? Would she scream and struggle? Or would she melt into his arms?

Belatedly her sense of humour came to her rescue. The security guard would object strenuously to such a course of action, not so much at she herself being borne from the studio as at his rubies. *Settle down, Moira*, she told herself. *This is strictly business ... remember?*

Patrick swept her a deep bow. 'So the virgin has vanished,' he drawled. 'You shouldn't have to act at all this afternoon.'

If she were to tell him the truth, he would laugh in her face. Her nostrils flared. 'That depends on whether we have to be pleasant to each other or not, doesn't it?'

Peter rushed up to them, his red hair standing on end. 'That's exactly the look we want! You're going to the opera or the ballet on a winter's night—two very sophisticated people who've only just met and who strike sparks off each other. The sex war. Seduction and antagonism. Love and hate. You know the kind of thing, Moira.'

'I'm sure she does,' Patrick offered smoothly.

Peter ignored this aside in a way Moira could only envy. 'We're going to use fans to blow your cloak open, Moira, we want to see your legs. And we'll have snow. Great colours—red, black, and white. Fantastic.'

The fan was waist-height and very powerful; the snow was shredded styrofoam, thrown in front of another fan from the top of a ladder by Peter. It should have been difficult for Moira to look seductive and antagonistic when her knees were cold and styrofoam was being blown in her face; but somehow it wasn't. The sparks were undoubtedly there, and while the tilt of her chin was haughty, her mouth was a sultry curve. Patrick's eyes smouldered into hers, the message one of blatant sexuality; he had the arrogant bearing of a man who knows he will get what he wants before the night is over.

For nearly two hours they strutted and posed under the lights, with periodic breaks for Peter to sweep up the drifts of styrofoam on the floor and clamber up his ladder again. Finally, after going through five rolls of film, Derek pronounced himself satisfied. Moira knew him well enough to know he was more than satisfied, but it was not Derek's style to dole out lavish doses of praise.

'Is that it?' Patrick queried.

Peter turned off the fans. 'That's it. Nine o'clock tomorrow. Autumn in the morning, summer in the afternoon.'

Moira closed her eyes, stretching her neck and back and rotating the stiffness from her shoulders. It would be heaven to get out of these shoes ... Then hands seized her shoulders through the stiff folds of the cloak, and her eyes snapped open. It was Patrick, his face intent with purpose, blue flames in his eyes. 'I've been wanting to do this all day,' he said, moving his hands to clasp her body, lowering his head to hers.

She was too surprised to protest ... or maybe, deep within her, she too had been waiting for this all day. His mouth was very sure of itself, his lips warm to the touch. Her own soft and willing. Her lashes drooped to her cheeks, her fingers sliding around his neck. Against his thick black hair the ruby sparkled and throbbed with a life of its own.

'Miss Tennant, I must have the jewels. Please, Miss Tennant ... sir. The rubies.'

Not hurrying, Patrick raised his head, speaking only to Moira. 'I rather thought you'd be willing ... We must do that again sometime, when we have less of an audience.'

Dazedly Moira looked around her. The security guard had planted himself only a foot away from her, Gwendolyn was regarding them with misty-eyed approval and Derek was giving them a cold-eyed stare. Peter, of course, was busy somewhere else. 'Oh . . . the rubies,' she stammered. 'Of course. You can take them now.'

When Patrick released her, she felt as though part of herself had been torn away. Her fingers were not quite steady as she undid the safety catch on the ruby brooch at her throat; but Patrick did not see this. Patrick had turned away and was handing an open-mouthed Gwendolyn the leather cloak as if nothing had happened. He headed for the changing room without a backward glance.

If Gwendolyn said anything, anything at all, she, Moira, would scream. Pulling the cloak around her, Moira walked to the cubicle with her nose in the air, looking every bit as disdainful as Derek could have wished. She took her time getting changed. When she finally emerged, in blue jeans and boots again, Patrick had gone. She quickly said her goodbyes to the rest and fled down the stairs.

It was rush hour, and still raining. She waited fifteen minutes for a cab, which then took the best part of an hour to get to her house. Aching with tiredness, horribly depressed, Moira cooked a light meal, read for an hour, and went to bed. She did not even allow Patrick's name to cross her mind, let alone anticipate what might happen the following day.

As it happened, the next morning passed off very smoothly. Gwendolyn arrived with large sprays of dried beech leaves and a beautiful, if not very bright, golden-haired retriever, the combination of which were to supply a suitably autumnal mood. Moira was to be The Girl Next Door, all glowing skin and cheerful smiles. Her canvas buckled pants were worn with a gloriously chunky sweater and Italian loafers, while Patrick sported a masculine version of the same outfit with hiking boots. The dog, by gazing at them both with indiscriminate adoration, seemed to keep at bay any antagonism or tension. Derek actually managed a smile at the end of the shooting; Peter was more relaxed than Moira had ever seen him.

The afternoon, however, was disastrous. Peter's idea of summer was to expose the maximum amount of skin; Moira gasped when she saw the bikini she was supposed to wear. 'Gwen, I'll be arrested for indecent exposure.'

'Arrested for causing a riot, more likely.'

'What's Patrick wearing?'

'Less than you.'

'Oh no! Couldn't I wear a cover-up?'

'You've done swimsuit ads before, Moira. What's wrong with you?'

It was one thing to wear an evening gown that exposed glimpses of her legs to Patrick, quite another to wear three scraps of sequined fabric that exposed her whole body. And to know that he would be equally exposed . . . 'For goodness sake, tell Derek to put the heat up,' Moira said irritably. 'I don't want to catch pneumonia.' She began to strip off her clothes.

Sharon patiently applied body make-up with a pan stick and baby oil, then wet Moira's hair as if she had just emerged from the sea. Taking a deep breath, feeling her hair damp and cold on her neck, Moira stepped into the studio.

Patrick, who was standing talking to Derek, looked no more pleased with the situation than she was. His navy-blue briefs were indeed brief; he had a beautiful body, as muscular as she had somehow expected, lean of hip and taut of chest. Dark hair funnelled to his navel while a slender gold chain encirled his neck. *A gift from a woman*, she thought sickly. *It has to be.*

Peter had spread heavy white canvas on the floor and supplied two massive, multicoloured beach balls; fortunately Gwendolyn had returned the dog at lunch time. Oblivious to any constraint between his two models, Peter said briskly, 'Okay. We've had the sweet young thing, the sophisticate, and the wholesome college-type. Now we want the siren. Pull out all the stops, Moira. We want this to be just as sexy as the winter scene, but now you're willing. Get the picture?'

She had the picture all right. 'Don't you think it would be sexier if I wore some kind of cover-up? It could be see-through.'

'Nope.' He gave her figure an impersonal glance as if it was nothing but a set of measurements on a page. 'You've got a fabulous body. Let's show it. Patrick, you lie down propped against the beach ball. Lean on one elbow. Moira, I want you to lie across him, your head thrown back. Sharon, comb her hair straight, will you? Let's go.'

Patrick muttered an expletive under his breath which only Moira was near enough to hear. He was echoing her sentiments exactly, although she was damned if he was going to know that. Avoiding his eyes, she waited until he had settled himself on the canvas, his legs stretched out, then lay back over his hips, one knee raised.

'Head back and close your eyes, Moira. Fix her hair, Sharon. How's that, Derek?'

'We'll start off with that.'

The polaroids were shot and minutely observed. Then Derek adjusted one of the lights before taking two shots with the flash. Peter interrupted him. 'It's not right,' he said discontentedly. 'Moira, you look stiff as a board. It's summer, for God's sake. The sun's shining, you're lying on the beach with your lover. Look as though you're enjoying it rather than enduring it, will you?'

Moira took another long breath. Patrick's hip bone was digging into her spine, the sinewed warmth of his flesh scorching her back. His muscles were rigid; she knew he was just as tense as she.

She tried. She forced herself to relax, she pasted what she hoped was a mysteriously sensual smile on her lips, and let her fingers trail suggestively down Patrick's thigh.

'That's better,' Peter said grudgingly. 'Patrick, you've

just made love with the woman. You're satiated, not desperate. Put one hand across her body. Just under her breasts.'

She heard Patrick's indrawn hiss of breath, and with every nerve-ending in her body felt the heaviness of his hand trail over her ribs to rest near the sequined triangles of fabric. Her body sprang to life; she ached for his hand to move upwards and cup her breast, to caress it slowly and lingeringly. Terrified that her longing was written in her face, she schooled her features to blankness and lay absolutely still.

'For God's *sake*!' Peter exclaimed. 'Moira, what the hell's wrong with you? You're not being raped—you're willing!'

Tell me about it. 'All right, all right,' she snapped.

'Put your hand on his leg again.'

She did so, and felt Patrick's flesh tense in rejection. Without conscious thought she twisted her neck to look straight up at him and said in a strangled voice, 'Patrick, I hate this just as much as you do. Let's get it over with as quickly as we can. Please.'

Her appeal had startled him. His eyes were a turbulent mixture of emotions, none of which she could decipher. Then, infinitesimally, some of the tension left his body. 'You hate it, too?'

She nodded, her hair dank on her neck, praying he would not ask why she hated it.

'You're right—let's get it over with.' He gave her a quick, conspiratorial grin that was almost as devastating to her nerves as the hardness of his hand against her breast, and added, 'Think of it this way—we're in acting school. We've just been told to be two satiated lovers. As Peter would say, let's go.'

Her chuckle rippled through her frame, and with it a sense of deep relief. She flickered her lashes, pouted her lips and slid her body more closely into the angle of his. The heat of the lamps became the heat of the sun as her fingers teased the dark hair on his thigh.

'Great!' said Peter. 'You got it.'

The trouble was that for Moira it all very rapidly passed from the realm of acting to the realm of reality. She loved the smooth slide of Patrick's skin under hers. When she lay back on the canvas and he bent over her, his hand stroking her hip, she longed for him to kiss her; when they stood up and she threw herself back over his arm, she thrilled to the strength that he seemed to take for granted. She did not know whether to be glad or sorry when Derek announced, 'I've got enough. Unless there's anything else you want, Peter?'

'Nope. We got a great sequence of shots—although you both had me worried at the beginning.'

Patrick and Moira were still standing entwined, his arm about her waist, her palm cupping his shoulder. With an abruptness that shocked her, he pulled away. Her hand, of necessity, dropped to her side. He said harshly, 'Thank God that's over.'

She turned away, to her horror feeling tears prick at her eyes. As she stared at her painted toenails in apparent fascination, her hair fell forward, baring the nape of her neck.

Behind her Patrick gave a muffled exclamation. He pulled her round to face him, raising her chin with one hand as he gazed into her drowned eyes. 'I didn't mean to hurt your feelings, Moira. I hated that session for reasons we needn't go into now. But it was nothing you did. You were fine.'

'Oh. I see.' She swallowed, her mind suddenly blank. She believed him, but it did not seem to help the torment of emotion that he had aroused simply by touching her.

'What do you do on Sunday afternoons?'

She gaped at him, totally confused by the change of subject. 'I go to the Metropolitan Museum usually. Why?'

'Which section will you be in at three o'clock this Sunday?'

She blinked back the tears. 'The European galleries. The Dutch section.' She was systematically working her way through the entire collection.

'I'll meet you there.'

'Why?' she burst out.

Gently he put a finger on her lips. 'Don't ask so many questions. If you're free, we'll go out for dinner afterwards. Now I'd better go and get dressed, or Gwendolyn's going to have us married off. See you Sunday.'

She stood riveted to the spot, shivering a little now that Derek had switched off the lamps. Patrick wanted to see her again. Despite all the undercurrents of the past two days, he wanted to see her again. In less than forty-eight hours they would spend an afternoon and an evening together. Nobody else around. Just the two of them. She gave Derek a brilliant smile which he managed to ignore, and hurried off to the cubicle.

CHAPTER FOUR

On Saturday Moira had an assignment on location in Boston. She took the shuttle from La Guardia and a cab to the Commons, where for five hours under a pale winter sun she was photographed in a selection of high-fashion winter coats. She sprawled across a bench, splayed herself against the trunk of a tree, swaggered across the grass, and gazed superciliously at the sky, all the while trying to ignore the comments of the crowd that had gathered to watch. Some of the remarks were funny; others were downright obscene.

By the time it was all over, she simply wanted to get home. Not bothering to eat, she flew back to New York, threw together a sandwich in her kitchen, changed, and went to the Lincoln Center with Anton. The programme was entirely twentieth-century music, much of it atonal, and, to her ears, devoid of melody or interest. When she finally got back to the town house, she felt as though the day had been going on forever.

Moira slept late the next morning. When she awoke, she lay in bed for a while, hugging to herself the thought that she would see Patrick today. What would their meeting be like? How would he behave? Would he kiss her again, as he had in the studio?

Eventually she got up and had a leisurely bath, giving careful thought to what she would wear. She did not want to look like Moira Tennant, famous model. She wanted to look ordinary: a young woman meeting a friend at the art gallery. She eventually chose a plain coat of dark plum over a gathered skirt with a floral design in black, plum and purple, her silk blouse of a shade between black and purple. She added a simple gold chain and earrings and tight black leather boots. Her make-up was discreet, her hair a smooth chignon gathered into a dark velvet ribbon.

With an unaccustomed lack of confidence, she gazed at herself in the mirror. Would Patrick see her as a real person? Or would he see only the elegant, successful model who was scarcely real at all?

She kept firmly to her normal routine, leaving the house a little after one, walking across town to Fifth Avenue, then north along the boundary of Central Park. The sun was poking between the clouds. The pigeons, at least, seemed to think spring was coming, for they were gabbling and cooing as they searched for scraps on the sidewalk. Pedestrians were strolling rather than rushing, and even the traffic seemed less raucous than usual. Moira jogged up the stone steps in front of the huge colonnades of the museum, paid her admission fee, and went uptairs.

Immediately she was transported into another world. She loved the Dutch paintings of three centuries ago: Ruisdael's arched skies and sweeping wheatfields, Hobbema's more intimate village scenes, Vermeer's deceptively simple, intensely moving interiors. She was standing lost in thought in front of a Rembrandt when Patrick walked into the room. If her aim had been to look ordinary she had not succeeded, for amidst the casual flow of visitors in and out of the room, she stood out immediately. Her profile, delicate yet distinct, was etched against the far wall, while her bearing was unconsciously one of a grace and dignity that had little or nothing to do with what she was wearing. For a minute or two the dark-suited man stood in the archway watching her as intently as she was regarding the painting. Then he crossed the room to stand at her side, giving the portrait a cursory glance. He said in deliberate challenge, 'You don't look at all bored today.'

Moira turned her head, regarding him thoughtfully. 'No. I'm not.' Unexpectedly her eyes twinkled. 'I have a feeling it might be difficult to be bored with you around.'

He did not smile back. 'Why do you come here, Moira?' With a taut gesture he indicated the masterpieces hanging on the walls around them. His voice was harsh. 'What have all these got to do with you?'

She fought down dismay at his mood. 'Perhaps I come because this place restores my sense of proportion.'

'I would have thought it would have emphasised all the worst in what you do.'

So he wanted a fight, did he, she thought grimly, her vision of a peaceful and intimate Sunday afternoon rapidly fading away. Very well. She'd be happy to oblige. 'You're determined to disparage me, aren't you?' she retorted. 'Does it affront your male ego that I probably make as much money as you do and, in my own way, am just as well-known?'

'No! That's the least of my concerns——'

'I don't believe you.' She glared at him. 'I threaten you, don't I, Patrick Casey? Because I'm an independent woman. Because I don't need a man for economic or psychological security—I can make it on my own. You'd prefer me to be fluttering around begging you to rescue me from the horrors of being a woman alone. Well, if that's what you want, you'll wait a long time!'

In an apparent change of subject he said tersely, 'I've never married. Does it occur to you to wonder why?'

'Not at all. Why should it?' she answered with a complete disregard for truth.

'It was because I couldn't bear the thought of having someone else depending on me for everything. An independent woman is exactly what I want. What I can't stand is seeing you revolve your days around what colour eyeshadow to wear and whether your hem should be three inches below the knee or ten inches above. It's so bloody trivial! Alongside all this,' again his gesture encompassed the paintings around them, 'it doesn't mean a damn thing.'

She kept her voice level with an effort. 'I already told you this place keeps things in proportion for me.'

'Proportion! I should think it would make you run a mile.'

She lost her temper completely. 'Unfortunately we aren't all lucky enough to have jobs as significant and meaningful as yours!' she raged. 'If everyone went around writing plays, where the hell would we be? Let me tell you something——' Her eyes blazed into his. 'I came from the slums of a coal-mining town to this city, and I made it to the top. Don't you *dare* belittle what I've done!'

Someone said very politely, 'Excuse me, please, madam. I must ask you to keep your voice down.'

Oh, no . . . Slowly Moira turned her head. She and Patrick were the centre of attention for a considerable group of people, including the security guard who had spoken.

A teenager with spiky orange hair said to her companion, 'That's the model. You know, the one who sells Revlon.'

'Yeah. I saw her on TV last night.'

A young boy piped up, 'He writes plays. My dad took me to one.' He addressed Patrick. 'Is she going to be in your next play?'

'I am not!' Moira answered roundly. 'I'm not *that* desperate.'

'So you are desperate,' Patrick said calmly. 'I knew you were.'

She took a very deep breath and counted to ten before expelling it. Smiling brightly at their audience, she then took Patrick's arm and said with considerable aplomb, 'The fight's over. We are now going to look at paintings like two normal civilised people.' Just as firmly she turned her back on them and addressed her attention to the Rembrandt.

'Well done,' murmured Patrick. 'Any encore?'

She hissed nastily, 'You're a born performer, that's your problem. You can't do anything unless you've got an audience.'

'I promise you that our next fight will be staged when we are totally alone.'

'Why does it have to be staged at all? Why *do* you keep fighting me, Patrick?'

'Oh, I can't tell you that now. This is only Act One. Very bad theatre to give away too much too soon.'

'It's a good thing there aren't any priceless sculptures in here,' she seethed. 'Because if there were, I'd throw one at you.'

He gave her a lazy smile. 'Then we'd be chucked out for sure. You know, the first time I saw you I didn't think there was a genuine emotion in you. I'm delighted to be proved wrong. You're a hotbed of emotions. A veritable Vesuvius.'

'Why should you care what I'm like?'

He grinned at her. 'Because I fell in love with you the moment I laid eyes on you, of course.'

She grimaced. 'Oh sure,' she said irritably. 'If that's the way you behave when you fall in love, I'd hate to be someone you disliked on sight.'

'You'll never know what that's like, will you?' She was still clutching his sleeve. He rested his hand on hers, playing with her fingers, and added, 'Don't you think we should at least pretend to look at some paintings? That's what we came for, after all.'

She pulled her hand free. 'I can't look at paintings while you're doing that—it's too distracting.'

'Good! The effect is entirely mutual, by the way.'

With atrocious timing Moira remembered the heat of his skin on her back, and blushed. Blushing was becoming a habit with her. Staring at the Rembrandt, which depicted a middle-aged man in Arab dress, she said, 'It isn't chance that you found me in front of this particular painting at three o'clock.'

'Oh?' He gazed at the portrait. 'There's a message?'

'Indeed.' She paused, picking out her words. 'His clothing is magnificent, isn't it? That wonderful turban and the gold sheen of his robe. But it's his face which holds one's attention rather than his clothes. He always looks perplexed to me. Worried about something. And so very real ... you see, under whatever clothes and make-up I happen to be wearing, I'm just as real as he is. You're only seeing the gold robe and the jewels. Not the person underneath.'

Very deliberately Patrick brought his hand up, cupped her face in his palms, and kissed her mouth. As she gazed at him, dumbstruck, he said quietly, 'I suppose that's how you must have seen it. I'm sorry, I know I'm not behaving very well. It's been a long time since I've been in love, I'm not used to it.'

For a moment Moira looked just as perplexed as the man on the canvas beside her. 'I do wish you'd stop saying that.'

'You think it's a line I should save until later on?'

'I'm not sure it's a line I want to hear at all.'

'Oh, it's got to be said sooner or later. That I do know.'

'Maybe you should have more respect for your audience.'

He smiled, his blue eyes so full of warmth that she was bemused. 'I'm beginning to have a great deal of respect for her. And now I think we should take a look at Rembrandt's Aristotle. His *Simeon in the Temple* is here too, I believe. Have you seen *The Adoration of the Magi* in London?'

She had. They wandered around the room, discussing their favourite artists and learning about each other's travels. Moira was glad of the respite. She had no idea whether Patrick was joking or serious when he said he was in love with her; she suspected the former, although surely the sweetness of his smile had not been an act. He seemed to have the ability within the span of only a few minutes to evoke a whole range of emotions in her, from rage to a breathless delight, so that she felt more like a teenager than a supposedly poised and sophisticated career woman. It was very confusing. Margarita would be pleased to see her at such a loss. Margarita would have applauded the scene in front of the Rembrandt.

When they left the gallery they walked towards 59th Street through the park, arm in arm, exchanging reminiscences about the European countries they had visited, he as a struggling young writer, she as a fledgeling model. They had a drink in the bar of one of the fashionable hotels near Fifth Avenue, then walked to a restaurant off 52nd Street that Patrick knew. The restaurant was warm and cosy after the darkness outside; seated in a velvet-padded booth, they had almost complete privacy. Moira found herself downing a second Bloody Caesar and said uncertainly, 'I normally don't drink much. If we have wine as well, you'll probably have to carry me out.'

'Don't tempt me. The asparagus vinaigrette is delicious, and I'd recommend the tournedos and the veal escalopes.'

The entire meal was delicious. As the courses progressed, Patrick and Moira discussed politics, music, and religion, fencing with each other the whole time, giving nothing away, playing a game each could sustain with ease. It was not until the waiter had left them with coffee and liqueurs that a silence fell. Patrick broke it by saying with a lightness that did not deceive Moira in the least, 'Now that we've proved what brilliant conversationalists we are, tell me about yourself, Moira.'

'That's a large order.'

He smiled crookedly. 'In the heat of our last argument you mentioned a coal-mining town. Why don't you begin there?'

'That's a large order, too.' She stirred some cream in her coffee, feeling as though she was on the verge of a monumental decision. She had accused Patrick of not seeing the real person under the make-up ... but how willing was she to reveal the real person? Except with Margarita, she rarely discussed her background. To share it with Patrick meant a huge step towards intimacy. Troubled, she looked up at him, the candlelight flickering over her face.

'You can trust me,' he said gently. 'I'll never put you in a play, and I avoid the press like the plague.'

'I wasn't thinking of that.'

'So you recognise that this is the moment when we either remain acquaintances or move forward to become something more.' He nodded slowly. 'I wondered if you would.'

'I have a great many acquaintances—but very few friends. It's a big step for me.'

'You're not ready to take it yet, are you?'

'No,' she said in a small voice. 'Not yet.'

He shifted in his seat. 'I'm pushing you, I know. I can't seem to help it.'

The wine had loosened her tongue. 'You can't be in love with me, Patrick—you only just met me. And all we've done is fight.'

His gaze was disturbingly intense. 'I can't explain what's happening. All I know is that when I saw you walking across the room at Ted's party, I had this gut feeling that you were important to me. You mattered. I can't explain it or justify it. Equally I can't deny it. When I say I'm in love, I'm just using the popular phrase that everyone uses. You tell me what it means—I don't know.'

She managed a weak smile. 'I'm not what you'd call an expert on the subject.'

'Despite the way the press is always trying to link me up with one actress or another, neither am I. I want you to know that, Moira. I'm not in the habit of going up to beautiful women and harassing them just to get a reaction.' He leaned forward, taking one of her hands in his and holding it tightly. 'If there's one thing I've learned over the years, it's to trust my gut reactions. I don't know yet what I want of you. But I want something. And it's not to be taken lightly.' He broke off, staring down at their clasped hands. 'I'm making one hell of a poor job of this. You'd think that as a man who makes his living with words, I'd be able to spout great gobs of poetry and have you swooning at my feet. Whereas all I can do is talk about gut reactions. Nothing very romantic in that.'

Moira said meekly, 'I prefer the gut reactions to the poetry. Any day of the week.'

He looked full at her. Her hair gleamed in the wavering flame of the candle; her eyes were as dark as her blouse, shy, frightened, yet touchingly honest. With a gesture that tore at her heart, he lifted her hand to his mouth and buried his lips in her palm. Featherlight, her free hand reached out and touched his hair, then withdrew so quickly that the caress might have been imagined.

For a moment Patrick strained her hand to his cheek. He said hoarsely, 'I'd be hell to live with. I hate to sound so bloody artistic, but I've never been able to work from nine to five, five days a week, like everyone else. When I'm working on a play and it's going well, I'm oblivious to the rest of the world. When it's not, watch out. I can't write in New York, I've never been able to. I spend about a third of my year here, dealing with agents and directing. When I'm writing I live in a little village in New Brunswick that's miles from anywhere ... I can't analyse the creative process, Moira. Maybe I'm scared to, in case it goes away. I do know that when a new work's on my mind, I'm as absent-minded as the proverbial professor. I forget meals. I forget appointments. I find myself in the middle of a shopping mall with no idea what I came for. Sounds silly, I suppose, but it drives me crazy sometimes, and I'm sure it would drive someone else crazy.'

She digested this in silence. Finally she said, 'Are you warning me off?'

'God, no. But I am trying to give you some idea of what my life is like ... Right now I can feel the next play building in my mind—it's like pressure in a steam engine. So I'll have to go back to New Brunswick fairly soon.'

She suddenly felt icy-cold. 'You'll be leaving the city?' she stammered.

'I'll have to. There's no real choice. I have to get the play down on paper and I can't do it here.'

Moira picked up her liqueur glass, drained it in one gulp, and choked. *At least*, she thought fuzzily, as she buried her face in her white linen napkin, *that's an excuse to have tears in my eyes*. It also gave her an excuse to flee to the washroom to fix her make-up. As she powdered her face and brushed on lip gloss, the only coherent conclusion that she could reach was that she was not bored. Slightly drunk, totally confused, frightened out of all proportion at the prospect of Patrick leaving her life as precipitately as he had entered it . . . but not bored.

Patrick was standing waiting for her when she went back into the dining area. After he had paid the bill, he helped her on with her coat and they went back outside, where he said abruptly, 'Shall we get a cab? Or would you rather walk?'

Sensing in him a need for action, she said casually, tucking her arm in his, 'Let's walk. It's not that far.'

And walk they did. Patrick strode along as if the entire New York police force was after him; Moira was flushed and breathless when they reached the cul-de-sac by the river. They had scarcely talked the whole way, which had given her mind plenty of time to work. When they reached her navy blue front door with its brass knocker, she said as nonchalantly as if she did this every night of the week, 'Why don't you come in for a minute? I'll make some more coffee.'

She was not at all surprised when he accepted instantly. She ushered him in, flicked on the hall lightswitch, and turned to take his coat. With a muffled groan he put his arms around her, straining her close, and kissed her as if he could never have enough of her.

Moira clung to him, less from passion than from a desire to remain standing. For as his mouth moved against hers and his tongue teased her lips open, the floor seemed to sway under her feet and the hall light grew as brilliant as fire, as golden as sunshine. He had no need of poetry, she thought muzzily. He had only to kiss her and the heavens sang . . . That her own hunger should be as direct and primitive as his shocked her. But she would have been less than honest had she not also admitted that it delighted her.

When Patrick finally released her, her blouse was tugged from her waistband, her chignon was considerably less sleek, and her eyes were dazzled in a way no amount of make-up could have achieved. She said helplessly, 'Oh, Patrick . . .'

He brought her hand to his left side, pressing it against his chest so she could feel the hard pounding of his heart. He said harshly, 'I should be wooing you with soft music and roses. But there's no time. Why couldn't I have met you in January?'

There was no answer to that. 'I can do without the roses.' Her mouth quirked. 'Now if you were to offer me daffodils . . .'

'I never want to see another daffodil again!'

'You really hated those sessions, didn't you?'

'Yeah . . . gazing dotingly into your eyes when I want to is one thing. Being told to do it for the benefit of the readers of a fashion magazine is another. Particularly when we were both half-naked.'

'Nine-tenths, you mean,' she said feelingly, dropping her eyes. 'I—I thought you were repelled by me. That you thought I was cheap or ugly or something.'

'Repelled—darling Moira!' His eyes were reckless with laughter. 'You're a big girl, I shouldn't have to explain this to you. The entire time you were in that so-called swimsuit, I wanted to throw the rest of them out of the window and make love to you right there on the floor. Being a man, that kind of urge tends to show—all the more when you're wearing as little as I was. The reason I was being so bloody-minded was that I did not want my sexual craving for you recorded for posterity. Particularly by that cold fish Derek.'

'Oh.' Her cheeks felt as though they were on fire. 'I never thought of that,' she stuttered. 'You must think I'm terribly naive.'

'I think it's rather sweet that you're so modest. Ugly—my God! Nothing could be farther from the truth . . . You're blushing, Moira.'

'I go on and off like a neon light whenever you're

within ten feet of me,' she complained. 'It's very disconcerting.'

'I'm flattered.' He paused. 'Nevertheless, I'm not going to take the risk of taking my coat off—unless you want to be ravished on the carpet?'

His words were teasing, his eyes were not. She said soberly, 'I'm not ready for that yet. Despite the evidence of that kiss.'

'As long as I know you want me as badly as I want you, I can wait. I think. When can I see you again—tomorrow?'

She said despairingly, 'I fly to Phoenix tomorrow morning for three days. Golfing outfits and sportswear.'

'Hell.' Patrick raked his fingers through his hair, making it stand on end, so that he looked like a small boy who has been deprived of his favourite toy.

Swallowing a laugh, Moira offered, 'You could meet the plane when I come home. If you wanted to.'

'Write down the flight number and the time. I'm lousy at remembering things like that.'

She led him into the living room and rummaged in the desk for her ticket. She wrote the information on a scrap of paper and gave it to him.

'What's the name of your hotel? Put that down as well.'

Obediently she did so. He put the paper in his wallet, said briefly, 'I like this room—it suits you,' and went back towards the front door. 'Good night, Moira.'

She whispered, 'Good night,' wanting him to kiss her again, knowing if he did, she would be lost.

As if he had read her mind, he said, 'It is too soon, you're right. Just tell me one thing—you're not involved with anyone else, are you?'

'No.'

'Thank God for that.' He raised a hand in quick salute. 'Sleep well.'

The door shut behind him and Moira was left alone, still in her plum coat, a tendril of hair brushing her cheek. Three days until she would see him again. It seemed like a lifetime.

CHAPTER FIVE

PHOENIX basked in the sunshine; against a clear blue sky the rust-red mountains encircled the city. In the desert the cacti were in bloom, red and yellow and pink, the flaming blossoms of the Ocotillo waving in the breeze. Scattered over the golf course the ribbed and branched giant Suguaro stretched forty feet into the air.

Two years ago, or even twelve months ago, Moira would have been delighted to have been in Pheonix, still new enough to the game to be impressed by the luxurious accommodations and the manicured surroundings. But this year was different. She resented being sent away from New York and Patrick for three long days. She inwardly fumed at the fussiness of the art director, who wore pink shorts and a diamond earring. She fretted through five-course meals in the vast dining room of the Arizona Biltmore, and in the splendour of her suite paced back and forth in an agony of loneliness. She was tired of having her life controlled by someone else. Tired of being at the agency's beck and call, and of assuming whatever personality the photographer required. Tired of modelling clothes that most of the population could not afford. Tired of spending hours in front of the mirror. Tired of smiling. Always smiling. Hour after hour. Day after day. Beautiful Moira Tennant ... glamorous Moira Tennant ... elegant Moira Tennant ... how she hated them all.

It was midnight on the second night when she stopped her pacing in front of the mirror in her bedroom to stare at her own exquisite reflection as if she had never seen herself before. It was not herself she hated, she thought numbly. It was her job.

For eight years she had revolved her entire life

around her career. Driven by ambition, she had worked her way to the top, until her face was known in every city across the country and her name alone was enough to sell a product. She was a success. She had achieved the American Dream. But she was also burned out. The challenge had gone. There was nothing left to achieve. She had become a victim of her own aspirations, a product of her own needs. Margarita was right. Over the years she had become Moira the model and had lost Moira the woman.

Cold fear gripped her. It was all very well to say she hated her job and did not want to do it any more. But it was her livelihood. It gave her an independence she cherished and would never want to lose. What else could she do instead? Nothing. She had no other talents or skills. She did not have a college degree. She was not trained for anything other than looking utterly beautiful in front of a camera.

She dropped down on the padded chair in front of the dresser, propping her chin in her hands. If she were the heroine of a book, she would discover in herself a latent—and brilliant—talent for painting or sculpture or writing, and overnight would transform herself into a celebrity of another sort, a successful artist. Her mouth twisted. Not a hope. Two or three years ago she had taken a series of evening classes in drawing and painting, sticking with them long enough to recognise, ruefully, that if she had gifts, they were not orientated towards pencil or paint brush. As for writing, her weekly letters to her parents in the little coal-mining town in Cape Breton were enough of a chore that the thought of starting an eighty-thousand word novel filled her with terror. And long ago, as a teenager, she had discovered that the brevity of poetry was in no way related to any ease of production.

All of which led her back to the one thing she could do, and do superlatively well: model. The way she felt right now it would be wonderful to tell the bejewelled art director what he could do with his pink shorts, to catch the first plane back to New York, and get the agency to remove her from its books. But she could not do that. And until she could come up with a viable alternative she was trapped.

She reached for her cleansing cream and began removing her make-up, her movements automatic. There was one alternative, the one Margarita had suggested. She could take a holiday. Go away for a month or two and rest. Get off the treadmill of fashion shows, travelling, and television commercials. As somebody or other had once said, invite her soul.

Her hands stilled. She would do it. She'd check her schedule as soon as she got home and she'd refuse any new bookings until she had two months free. *Free*. She was smiling at herself, a rather strange smile because she had removed the lip gloss from her upper lip and not the lower. But it was a better smile than she had given the photographer all day. Quickly finishing her task, she went to bed and instantly fell asleep.

The telephone bell was part of a confused dream in which Moira was yelling at the secretary in the agency to cancel all her bookings; the secretary, however, was far more interested in answering the four other phones which kept ringing on the desk. Struggling awake, Moira flailed out with her arm, knocked over a glass of water on the bedside table and grabbed the receiver. 'Hello?' she mumbled.

'You're surely not asleep?' said Patrick.

The alarm clock said ten minutes past two. 'Why wouldn't I be?'

'At ten o'clock in the evening? I almost didn't phone, I figured you'd be out partying.'

'Patrick, it's two a.m.'

There was a silence. 'Oh, hell. I got the time zones muddled. I told you I was forgetful.'

Moira snuggled under the covers, clasping the receiver to her ear and smiling sleepily into the darkness. 'That's all right.'

He said sharply, 'Are you alone?'

Across many hundreds of miles she poked her tongue out at him. 'Heavens, no—I'm having an orgy. Exotic dancers, transvestites, the works. Of course I'm alone.'

'What are you wearing?'

She blinked. 'A nightdress. Are you sure you're sober?'

'Stone cold sober. And frustrated. Describe it.'

'The nightdress? Well, it's got straps and a bodice and a skirt.'

'Come on, Moira, you can do better than that.'

The darkness, and the distance between New York and Phoenix, made her bold. 'It's pale grey chiffon. The bodice is minimal and the skirt see-through.'

His voice was husky. 'If I were there, you wouldn't be wearing it for long.'

She felt her body tingle to life. What would it be like to have Patrick beside her in the bed? To have him kiss her as he had kissed her in the hallway of her house, his tongue stroking her lip, her softness drawn to the hard length of his frame? She whispered shakily, 'I wish you *were* here.'

'I wish I were, too. I can't get you out of my mind.' He made a deliberate effort to be more matter-of-fact. 'What did you do all day?'

She described the art director's pink shorts and the photographer's annoyance because she had refused to drape herself around a very prickly cactus. 'We had to compromise on an ironwood tree. It was the last shot of the day, and we parted on less than friendly terms.'

'He'll be cross with you tomorrow because you'll have bags under your eyes from being awakened in the middle of the night by a lecherous playwright.'

'I never get bags under my eyes! Dark circles, maybe. Or romantic mauve shadows. But not bags.'

'You wait until I keep you awake all night making love to you. It'll be a different story then.'

She tried very hard to make her voice sound normal. 'No one could accuse you of disguising your intentions, Patrick.'

'Life's too short for that, Moira.'

'I—you frighten me sometimes.'

'I don't mean to. But I've got this sense of time rushing by. I'm going to head for New Brunswick soon, and then where will we be?' He answered his own question. 'A thousand miles apart, that's where.'

A holiday in New Brunswick ... the thought clicked into her brain and she almost spoke it out loud. But some vestige of caution kept her silent. He said irritably, 'I'd better end this conversation. I never did like the telephone, you can't see the other person's face—a deadly way to communicate. I'll be at the airport the day after tomorrow, and I swear I'll get the time right.'

'You mean you won't be two hours early or two hours late?' she teased.

'Scout's honour. Go back to sleep, darling Moira, and while you're in Phoenix don't embrace anything other than cacti.'

'That doesn't leave me much choice.'

'Good. Sweet dreams.' The connection was cut and she was left with the empty burring of the busy signal in her ear and a foolish grin on her mouth. She was also wide awake. After putting on a housecoat that was much more respectable than her nightdress, she ordered room service and sat cross-legged on the bed indulging in a luscious chocolate éclair and a cup of herbal tea. Events were moving too fast, she decided thoughtfully, as she tackled a cream puff from the selection of cakes she had requested. She was only just beginning to understand how her fierce drive to succeed had done her a disservice over the past few years by choking off nearly all her private life. She must now reassess her job, changing priorities to make more time for herself; possibly even changing direction in some way not yet clear to her. To have Patrick pressuring her into a sexual relationship at the same time—because that was all he wanted, wasn't it?—was too confusing. While one part of her wanted to tell him she would go to New

Brunswick for two months, and to hell with the consequences, the more cautious part of her personality was putting on the brakes. *Sort one thing out at a time, Moira. Maybe the reason you're so attracted to Patrick is because you're disillusioned with your career. Nature abhors a vacuum. All the energy you used to put into your job has got nowhere to go . . . so you're fancying you're in love.*

Slowly she drained the last of the tea from the silver pot into her cup. *In love? I'm not in love*, she protested.

Patrick, she was sure, saw her as a very experienced woman. Certainly her reputation and her looks must bolster that impression. It was, however, an impression very far from the truth. For if she were to be brutally honest, she would have to make another admission about the cost of her career: it had caused her to neglect her sexual needs. In classical fashion she had sublimated them in a drive for excellence and a frantic round of activities. So her attraction to Patrick was probably only a matter of hormones. Spring was in the air, she was bored to tears with her job, and ready to throw herself at the first attractive man who came along.

It was a depressing thought. So much for honesty, she decided wryly. So much for moonlight and roses . . . and daffodils.

Patrick must have been clairvoyant. When she saw him at La Guardia Airport the following evening he was standing head and shoulders over everyone else, clutching a huge bouquet of deep pink roses and baby's breath, the whole thing wrapped in cellophane. The pink was going to clash horribly with her suit and hat, both of which were acid yellow. Moira felt laughter rise within her, and a bubbling, irrational happiness. Then he caught sight of her and waved the bouquet vigorously in the air over the heads of the crowd behind the barrier. Recklessly she blew him a kiss.

The baggage carousel creaked into action, her

suitcase was eventually disgorged, and she edged her way towards the door. She could see now that he was wearing a very elegant three-piece pinstripe suit, his hair neatly combed, a daffodil stuck in his lapel. When she reached the doorway she stopped a foot away from him, feeling breathless, excited, and nervous. The crowd dropped away as if it did not exist. 'You look like a walking flower shop,' she remarked.

He swept her a low bow, depositing the bouquet in her arms. 'I'm on time, though.'

'So you are. Tell the truth—you got here two hours ago.'

'Fifteen minutes. Word of honour. Although every minute I waited for you seemed like an hour.'

She knew she was blushing again, but somehow it didn't seem to matter. 'The roses are beautiful—thank you.'

Hopefully he lowered his cheek. 'You could kiss me. Strictly as a gesture of gratitude.'

She kissed him full on the mouth, felt him pull her closer, and heard the crinkle of cellophane. 'The roses,' she babbled, pulling free. 'We'll ruin them.'

He took the bouquet from her arms, held it in one hand, and with his free arm drew her towards him. 'Let's try again.'

She had never been kissed quite so comprehensively before. Her hat was shoved back on her head, the pins pulling at her hair; her knees turned to jelly. When he raised his head, there was lipstick on his mouth. There was also a gratified silence from the remainder of the visitors behind the barrier. She stammered, 'We've got an audience again.'

'Then it's time for me to throw you across my black charger and ride off into the sunset.'

'Another of your dramatic exits.'

'Will you settle instead for a cab to my apartment?'

She straightened her hat and took the roses from him. 'What for?' she said bluntly.

'What a suspicious mind you have, darling Moira.

Dinner is awaiting you. I may be absent-minded, but I'm a marvellous cook. Filets de Poisson Bercy aux Champignons, and Soufflé à l'Orange.'

'Oh.'

He grinned wolfishly. 'After dinner I show you my etchings—which happen to be in my bedroom.'

At the look in his eye she became suddenly speechless. She pulled at the cellophane and hid her hot face in the silken petals of the roses.

Patrick picked up her case, took her elbow, and steered her towards the taxi rank. As they raced across the Triborough Bridge and down Franklin Roosevelt Drive, he chatted easily about the day he had spent with his publisher and agent sorting out financial matters. Moira listened obediently, cradling the roses, knowing if she were prudent she would go nowhere near Patrick's apartment. But prudency seemed to bear little relationship to what happened when he kissed her.

His apartment was undoubtedly expensive, for its location off Park Avenue was a prime one. But if Moira had hoped to gain many clues to the man from his surroundings, she was to be disappointed. The furniture was comfortable but undistinguished, the decorating scheme was bland, and there were no pictures on the walls, no plants, no ornaments or knick-knacks. The sole indication of the man who lived in the apartment was a profusion of books on the shelves.

Among them Moira spied a double gold frame containing photographs. While Patrick was getting her a drink she bent to look at them. On one side was a middle-aged couple, the man a heavier, older version of Patrick but every bit as good-looking, the woman's blue eyes crackling with intelligence and a barely concealed impatience to be done with this business of being photographed. Her greying hair was pulled into a knot on the top of her head, a severe style that emphasised her rather austere beauty. She and her husband—for Moira had no doubt these were Patrick's parents—were both wearing safari-styled shirts that were crumpled with wear.

Facing them in the double frame was a young auburn-haired woman with Patrick's blue eyes laughing into the camera. She was holding a baby on her hip; her head was resting on the broad shoulder of a bearded young giant with curly hair. In contrast to the other couple, who plainly viewed life as a serious business with serious responsibilities, they looked happy and carefree.

Patrick came back into the room with two glasses of pale dry sherry. Moira straightened, taking off her hat and putting it on the arm of a nondescript armchair. 'Your family?'

'Mum and Dad on the right. That was taken five or six years ago on one of their brief stops in this country.'

'They don't live in New Brunswick?'

'Not likely. They're archaeologists, passionately dedicated to their careers. At the moment they are in South America. They're always tearing off to some out-of-the-way place to dig it up. Among those who know about such things, their reputation is impeccable. As parents—well, let's say Kit and I were left a great deal to our own devices and those of various housekeepers and indigent relatives. Mum hadn't a motherly instinct in her, and made—as Dad was apt to say—no bones about it. I didn't really mind—I just got very independent very young. But Kit did. I think she always resented them for leaving her behind.' His face clouded. 'That's my sister Kit in the other photo.'

'She's younger than you?'

'By six years . . . she's having a hard time right now. Sandy—her husband—died of cancer six months ago, leaving her with two young children. They had another baby after that photo was taken.'

Moira made a tiny sound of distress. She had never met Kit, but something in the almost defiant happiness of Kit's smile had touched her. How terrible that that happiness had since been cruelly destroyed by the death of the man at her side. 'I'm so sorry,' she murmured, feeling the inadequacy of the conventional words even as she said them.

'My own theory is that because our parents were so rarely home, Kit grew up craving a relationship she could depend on. She used to trail after me everywhere. Then she met Sandy and transferred all her dependency on to him.' He smiled faintly. 'Sandy was big enough in body and spirit to cope with that. He was a fine man. But now he's gone and poor Kit is lost again. I'm glad she's got the children, because they force her to keep to some kind of routine. But I worry about her just the same ... She'll probably phone this evening. We keep in pretty close touch.'

'Where does she live?'

'Ontario. Sandy was the football coach at the University of Toronto. Once I go back to New Brunswick, I'll invite her and the kids to stay for a few days.'

New Brunswick again. Moira licked her lips and said brightly, 'How long before dinner?'

'Only a few minutes. Why don't I get you a vase for the roses?'

Moira was highly impressed by Patrick's cooking, and amused by his disclaimer that he had learned in self-defence. 'I went through the usual bachelor stage of eating out of cans, got thoroughly sick of it, and decided if I wasn't going to end up with malnutrition I'd better learn to cook.'

'Anyone who can make a soufflé has my wholehearted admiration. Do you cook like this all the time?'

'When I'm working on a play I revert back to opening cans. Can I get you more?'

'No, thanks. It was wonderful, but I've got to model evening gowns tomorrow and the next day, and I'll never get into them if I eat any more.'

'You work too hard, Moira.'

'That's why my friend Margarita says,' Moira replied equably.

'I'll have to meet her—we obviously share the same opinions.' Without changing his tone of voice he went on, 'Why don't you come to New Brunswick with me?

I'm going to have to leave in a few days.'

Her heart sank. It was too soon to give him an answer. 'I can't—I've got a job,' she said evasively.

'Take a break.'

'I can't, Patrick. I have commitments.'

'Change them. Get rid of them. You're high enough on the totem pole that you can do that.'

'It's not that simple.'

'I want to get you out of this city.'

'I belong here,' she retorted. But did she really believe that?'

'I hope not,' he replied grimly.

She was getting irritated. 'What's wrong with New York? Or should I say what's wrong with me?'

'It's one type of environment—but it's not the only one. There's a whole different world out there.'

'This is my world,' she said stubbornly. She pushed back from the table and went to stand by the window, edging aside the sheer curtain so she could see the panoply of lights that had been her home for eight years.

Patrick shoved back his chair, grabbed her shoulder, and spun her around to face him. 'You're suffocating in this city,' he said roughly. 'You're a product of it— glossy and smart and expensive—but only half real. Don't get me wrong, I admire what you've done. You've fought your way to the top of one of the most competitive businesses there is, and you've stayed at the top. You've got intelligence and guts. But you're only half alive, Moira!'

That she had been having identical thoughts herself was no help at all. She said tightly, 'We're fighting again.'

Briefly a flash of humour glimmered in his eyes. 'I said next time we fought there wouldn't be an audience—and there isn't.' His hands tightened on her and the humour vanished. 'You always look so goddamned perfect! Look at you—not a hair out of place, fingernails like talons, ultra-stylish clothes. I want to see you running down a hillside in your bare feet, your hair blowing in the wind. I want to put a chain of daisies around your neck and swim with you in the brook——'

'At this time of year?' she jeered.

The blue eyes were suddenly stone-cold. 'Don't push me too far, Moira Tennant.' Before she could guess his intentions his hands left her shoulders and fumbled in her hair, pulling out the pins that held her chignon in place.

She winced, trying to pull back. '*Stop* it!' But she was too late. Her hair fell to her shoulders in shining disarray.

He was breathing hard, and despite his immaculately tailored suit, did not look at all civilised. He looked, she decided furiously, thoroughly dangerous. She snarled, 'Don't you touch me again!'

'Maybe we should start with the clothes now—get them off and see if we get any nearer the real Moira Tennant. What are you like when you make love, Moira? Are you cool and in control, making all the right moves as gracefully as you pose in front of the camera? Or do you let go and moan with pleasure and dig your nails into a man's back?'

'You're not going to find out!' she spat, her eyes turbulent with rage.

'I already told you not to push me too far.' As he took a step closer to her, she held her ground, her chin stuck out. On their very first meeting she had known she would never beg for mercy from Patrick Casey; she was not going to start now.

The shrill of the telephone bell was pure anticlimax. Patrick's two-word comment verged on obscenity and would have been banned in most theatres. Fighting down a hysterical giggle, Moira said sweetly, 'You'd better answer it. It's probably your sister. Or one of the actresses.'

He pivoted on his heel and stalked across the room. The telephone was attached to the wall between the kitchen and the living room; Moira could hear every word. She pointedly turned her back and began pinning up her hair.

'Hello ... Kit, how are you, love?' There was a silence. Patrick's voice was sharp when he spoke again. 'When did it happen? ... I see. Is he still in hospital? ... Okay, love, take it easy. He's going to be all right, and that's the main thing. I'll phone the airport right away and see if I can get a flight tonight. If not, I'll come first thing tomorrow morning and go to the hospital with you ... Don't be silly, Kit, of course I'll come. How's the baby? ... Look, I'll call you back in an hour when I know what's going on. Will you be home by then? ... Take a cab, you shouldn't be driving when you're that upset. I'll be with you by tomorrow morning at the latest ... Okay, love, take care. See you soon.' Very slowly he replaced the receiver.

Moira was staring at him across the room, her own heart clenched with fear. There was no point in pretending she hadn't heard every word. 'What's wrong?'

'That was Kit. Peter—her elder son—fell into a highway culvert. Would have drowned if a teenaged girl hadn't heard him cry out. He's in the hospital being treated for shock and hypothermia. Kit's terribly upset, I'm going to fly up there as soon as I can.' He rummaged in the nearest drawer and pulled out the phone book.

'I'll start cleaning up the dishes.'

By the time she had them rinsed and stacked, Patrick had booked a seat on the last flight to Toronto. 'You pack,' Moira said. 'I'll arrange for a cab to pick you up here in twenty minutes.'

He dropped a kiss on her cheek in the abstracted manner of a husband for whom it was a long-familiar gesture. 'Thanks, Moira. You're a real help.'

Small words, but they made her glow with happiness. She called the car company and loaded the plates in the dishwasher as quickly as she could, afterwards turning it on and cleaning off the top of the stove. In eighteen minutes they were on the elevator going downstairs. Patrick said, 'Will you come out to the airport with me? I'd like your company.'

'Of course.'

'I'll pay for your cab back in.'

'No, you won't. I'm an independent woman—remember?'

They left the elevator and he pushed open the outside door. The cab was waiting for them. Patrick gave the driver their destination and sat back in the seat, reaching for Moira's hand and holding it in his own. 'Is that why we keep fighting?' he asked innocently.

'We keep fighting because we're *both* independent—not to say strong-minded.'

'The competitive phase of a relationship,' he rejoined. 'Circling around each other to see who's going to be boss.'

'Does anyone have to be?' She gazed at him guilelessly.

'Now there's a subject that could be discussed on many a winter evening.'

'You haven't answered the question.'

'Because I'm not sure of the answer. Fifty-fifty would work, you think?'

She wrinkled her nose. 'Sometimes it would probably have to be forty-nine to fifty-one.'

'Just as long as *you* weren't always the one who's forty-nine.'

'Exactly! Equal opportunities to be underdog.'

He grinned. 'Lots of chances there for us to keep right on fighting until we're both old and grey and too decrepit to fight any more.'

She responded drily, 'If you're in a village in New Brunswick and I'm in a town house in New York, it's going to be a little difficult to fight at all.'

Very quietly he said, 'Shall we try to work out an answer to that dilemma, Moira? Together?'

Her heart was hammering as fast as if she'd just run around Central Park. 'I—do you want to?'

'More and more every time I see you.'

'This is only the fifth time.' Then could have bitten off her tongue because he would now realise she had been keeping track.

'We make up in intensity what we lack in quantity. Fights are a great way to clear the air. By the way, we did rather leave the last one in the middle, didn't we? We'll have to continue it when I get back.'

'You're coming back? I thought you might go straight to New Brunswick.' Which neatly evaded the matter of the last fight.

'No. I've got to have another session with my agent, and I have to close up the apartment. I rent it furnished, but I like to leave it clean. I shouldn't be with Kit more than three or four days. She's upset right now, which is understandable so soon after Sandy's death, but I'm sure she'll have settled down in a day or two.'

'Tell me more about her children.'

'Peter's four, and the spitting image of Sandy as far as looks go. But he seems to have inherited more than his fair share of his grandparents' curiosity and urge to explore—which is no doubt why he came to fall into the culvert. He was either trying to figure out how it worked or else he was looking for the buried treasures of an Indian tribe. There'll be trouble between him and Kit in the next few years, I'm sure—he's already too independent for her taste. I think she's gone a bit overboard as far as mothering is concerned. Compensation for her own childhood, I expect. Sandy made sure she had a lot of other interests, but now that he's dead she's devoting all her energies to the two boys—not good for any of them. The baby's adorable, just over a year old, fat and placid. His name's Daniel.'

'You're very fond of them.'

'You said it. Typical doting uncle. In some ways I'd like to see Kit move to the Maritimes so I could be of more help to her and take the boys off her hands sometimes. But I'm sure she'd miss her friends in Toronto.'

'And you couldn't write in Toronto.'

'Probably not ... I don't know why I've got such a fixation on my place in New Brunswick. It's set in the hills between two tiny communities, one called Meadow, the other Pleasantvale. There are tree-clad, weathered mountains all around it with a sparkling trout stream and open fields dotted with sheep ... the birds sing, the wind blows in the trees, but otherwise it's so quiet that in winter you can almost hear the snowflakes fall. Perhaps it's the silence that I cherish the most.'

The cab was rattling over the bumps, two other lanes of traffic were racing in the same direction as they, horns were blaring, direction signals flashing; and all around them, as far as Moira could see, was a forest of lights from mile upon mile of skyscrapers, tenements, office buildings and warehouses. No empty black spaces where only trees grew. No sparkling streams where fish could weave between the rocks. Only a turgid, dirty river and a dim flickering of stars, their pale gleam blurred by the smog and the glow of light cast skyward by the city.

She could think of nothing to say. She sat quietly, very much aware of Patrick's hand cradling hers. Did she want him to be gone, so she could sink back into the cushioned comfort and security of the life she had built for herself? Or did she long for him to stay and bring her to life with his body and his words, both of which could rupture so easily the cocoon in which she had encased herself? She did not know the answers to her own questions. Blindly she stared out of the window.

They arrived at the terminal all too soon. Patrick paid the driver and gathered up his overnight bag and his raincoat. 'There's no point in you getting out—I'll have to go straight through security. Besides, you might as well take the same cab home. Take care of yourself, Moira. I should only be gone three or four days—but I'll get in touch with you tomorrow and let you know what's happening.' He gave her a quick, hard kiss on the mouth. 'I'll miss you.'

By the time she had stammered, 'I'll miss you, too,' he was out on the pavement. The door slammed shut behind him. She saw him raise a hand in salute, then vanish through the glass doors of the terminal. She gave her address to the driver in an emotionless voice and leaned back in the seat, closing her eyes against the sting of tears.

CHAPTER SIX

DETERMINED to clear some time for a holiday, Moira
spent an hour on the telephone the next morning before
leaving the house to model the evening gowns. It was a
very productive hour. The first person she phoned was
Gerald Wilmot, by far her favourite photographer and
the one with whom she did the majority of her studio
work; besides excelling at his craft he was the kindest
man she knew. After exchanging some of the usual in-
trade gossip with him, she said, 'Gerald, I'm trying to
free up six to eight weeks as soon as possible—I want to
take a holiday. What are the odds?'

'You're kidding.'

'No, I'm not. After eight years I'm due for a
holiday——'

'That's not what I meant. I got a call from the
hospital yesterday. I'm going in for a hip operation next
week. I hadn't mentioned it to you because they hadn't
expected to get me a bed for another two months. There
was a cancellation, though, so I'm booked for next
Wednesday. Because it's for health reasons I should be
able to delay most of the bookings—in fact, several of
them I'd scheduled early on purpose with the later
hospital date in mind. I'm sure I can clear you four
weeks, Moira. Maybe five—but not eight.'

'What's wrong with your hip?'

'Arthritis. At my age.' Gerald was in his forties.
'They can do wonderful things with artificial joints, so
I'm not too worried. I *was* worried about you—figured
you wouldn't be very happy to have your schedules
disrupted.'

'You don't need to worry about me. But I'm sorry
I'm getting a holiday at your expense. Which hospital
will you be in? I'll come for a visit.'

They chatted a few minutes longer. Then Moira dialled the agency, the television network, and two other photographers, one of them Derek, ruthlessly rearranging shootings. Because she had a well-earned reputation in the trade for dedication and co-operation, she found everyone but Derek co-operative in return, to the extent that she wondered why she had never tried to take a holiday before. Derek, however, was displeased. She said very pleasantly, 'Derek, this is the first time in eight years I have ever asked you to rearrange anything. If you can't manage to do it, then you can find another model.' She listened to him sputtering on the other end of the line with a faint smile on her face. Derek did not want anyone else. He wanted his name on shots of Moira Tennant.

He finally, grudgingly, gave her a date in six weeks' time and rang off with a pettish, 'Goodbye.' He did not wish her a happy holiday.

Moira sat there smiling at the living room wall. She had five weeks free. Five whole weeks. She might spend part of that time in New Brunswick, in a house on a hillside with Patrick. If he still wanted her. Somehow she was sure he did and somehow she was becoming increasingly sure that she wanted him.

The evening gowns ranged from a luxurious black panne velvet embroidered with gold and artificial jewels to a skimpy metallic knit that scarcely covered her nipples. In the former she was required to look aloof, in the latter wanton; by the time she got back to the town house, she decided she'd earned her day's wages. She cooked supper, watered her plants, flipped through a couple of Italian fashion magazines, and studied the latest report from her accountant, all the while waiting for Patrick to phone. Margarita phoned and they arranged to meet for drinks on Monday. Anton phoned to invite her to an all-Stravinsky programme in a couple of weeks; she liked Anton but could do without Stravinsky, so it was no great hardship to decline the invitation. She sensed Anton was surprised to hear about her prospective holiday, although he was too much of a diplomat and too non-possessive to ask if she was travelling alone.

Patrick did not phone.

Moira had a heavy workload lined up for the next day, so she went to bed relatively early, certain in her mind that she would be woken in the middle of the night by Patrick's call. But when she next opened her eyes it was to the shrill of the alarm, not of the telephone. She was puzzled and a little hurt by his defection, but sensible enough to realise that he may have walked into a very difficult situation at his sister's; a phone call to New York could well have been impossible.

The second day the evening wear ranged from the provocative to the bizarre. Moira slithered around the studio in gold lamé that left nothing to the imagination, then was wrapped like a parcel in bright red taffeta that was tied in an immense bow on her hip. The underdress was black; her lipstick and nails were black; the tips of her hair, spiked around her head, were sprayed red. As she thrust out her hip—the one with the bow—and stuck her nose in the air, she decided with an inward smile that she must get a copy of this one for Patrick. She had turned down an invitation from an artist who was very much in vogue in order to be home for Patrick's call this evening, and had been happy to do so.

She should have gone out with the artist, for once again Patrick did not phone, not that evening or the next. Nor was there a letter from him. Moira passed from disappointment to hurt to anger, which on the fifth day changed into fear. The plane had crashed, or he had had an accident. Something terrible must have happened that he had not got in touch with her. Only then did she realise with a sick clenching of her heart that she did not know his sister's married name or her address. Nor did she know Patrick's address or phone number in New Brunswick. Not to her surprise, a perusal of the atlas did not reveal the whereabouts of either Meadow or Pleasantvale.

At lunchtime on Monday she impulsively put on dark glasses and went to Patrick's apartment building. He did not answer the buzzer. The doorman had beady black eyes and an obsequious manner that changed into suspicion when she asked if Mr Casey was still away. 'Can't tell you that, madam.'

'I've been trying to reach him all week.' It was not hard to make her voice wobble. 'I'm afraid he might have had an accident.'

'Can't discuss the whereabouts of the tenants, madam. Against company rules.'

'Please, just tell me if you've seen him the last couple of days.'

Stonily the doorman said, ''Fraid I must ask you to leave, madam. See what the sign says?'

Moira looked over his shoulder, read 'No Loitering', and announced furiously, 'I shall complain to Mr Casey about your lack of co-operation when I see him.'

'After him, are you?' he leered. 'You're not the only one.'

Her natural inclination was to stamp her feet and scream at him. Instead she tilted her chin and marched out of the building with as much dignity as if she was wearing black panne velvet.

It was a relief to pour it all out to Margarita that evening when they met in the bar nearest to Margarita's office. 'It's so ironic,' Moira finished bitterly. 'Here I've arranged for five weeks off and had decided I'd go away with him for at least some of that time. I'd have sworn he wanted me to. But it's nearly a week now, and I haven't heard a word from him. He's probably having a wonderful time squiring the women of Toronto around while I sit home waiting for the phone to ring.' Viciously she stabbed an olive with a toothpick. 'More fool me.'

'A new role for you,' Margarita commented drily. 'I've never seen you this worked up over a man.'

'I don't get this worked up over ordinary men—only him.' Moira swallowed the last of her martini and ordered another. 'Maybe he does this with all his women. Convinces them he's falling for them in a big way and then conveniently disappears.'

'You mean the phone call from his sister was rigged?' Margarita said sceptically.

'Oh, I guess not—that was real enough. But he's obviously not in a hurry to get home.'

'Maybe his sister's in worse shape than he thought, so he's had to stay longer. There isn't anyone else to stay with her, is there? Her husband's dead and her parents are in South America, isn't that what you said?'

'Then why doesn't he *phone*?'

'The Ontario telephone system is on strike?' Margarita suggested.

'And the post office as well?'

'It doesn't seem very likely, does it?' Margarita ran her fingers through her shiny auburn hair; she looked exceptionally attractive in a jade green Chanel suit and gold costume jewellery. 'What are you going to do?'

Moira scowled at her martini, already half gone. 'Get drunk.'

'Not very productive. What else, Moira?'

'Go on holiday anyway,' Moira said defiantly. 'I'm not going to let anyone spoil my holiday. Not even Patrick Casey.'

'Good for you! Where will you go?'

Moira took another dangerously large gulp of her drink. 'Do you know, I haven't any idea. I think I'll just head north, up through New England.'

'At this time of year you'd be better off heading south.'

'I don't want to go to any big resorts—anywhere that I'm known. I just want to disappear and be plain Moira Tennant.'

Affectionately Margarita smiled at her friend. 'You'll never be plain anyone. But I understand what you mean . . . Why don't you visit your parents?'

Moira fiddled with her napkin, lining it up assiduously with the edge of the table. 'I should, I know. I haven't been home for months. But the last time I went I didn't fit in at all—I felt like a total stranger.'

'Maybe it would be different this time. After all, lately you've been having some problems with your own image, haven't you? You might find it easier to relate to your parents now.'

'Perhaps . . . How's the ad-man? Did he recover from appendicitis?'

Margarita accepted the change of subject with good grace. 'Most satisfactorily. I'm liking him more and more all the time, Moira. Having watched him go through his illness and recuperation, I've learned a good deal about him—more than I would have learned by dating him in the ordinary way.' It was her turn to play with her napkin, her eyes unaccustomedly vulnerable. 'He's wonderful with Shelley. He doesn't try to be a father figure, he's just himself. She really likes him.'

'Sounds as though you do, too.'

'Mmm. I—we haven't slept together yet. Apart from any other reasons, it's too soon after his operation. But I'm sure we will. I only hope I'm not being foolish getting involved with him. My marriage broke up and my affair with Bob didn't work out very well.'

'Third time lucky,' Moira said firmly, raising her glass, which seemed to be nearly empty again, in a toast.

She woke up the next morning with a hangover. Fortunately she had no appointments, for her eyes were bloodshot, her complexion pasty, and her stomach unreliable. Earlier in the week she had turned down two invitations for the evening, being certain that Patrick would be back. Determined not to spend another night waiting for the phone to ring, she leafed through the telephone book, made a call, and got herself a date. She ate, drank, and danced the evening away; although her partner thought she was having a wonderful time and was flattered, she knew better. Her mood swung from fury that Patrick could so easily go back on his word to a bitter pain that he had abandoned her. She did not understand how or why he should mean so much to her. She only knew that the thought of never seeing him again filled her with terror.

Wednesday, Thursday and Friday Moira worked exceptionally hard, having put forward one or two bookings in addition to her regular appointments. She planned to leave on Saturday afternoon. Friday evening she spent going through her wardrobe and perusing tourist literature about the New England states and the Maritime provinces. She also visited Gerald, who was already making short trips around his hospital room with the help of a cane.

When she woke up on Saturday morning and looked out of the window, she saw snowflakes falling from a leaden sky; the branches of the magnolia tree were etched in white; her tiny patch of grass was white-coated. Margarita was right: even though the snow was unseasonably late, this was still the time of year to go south, not north. But it was too late to change her plans. She'd find a country inn in New England and spend hours by the fireplace reading, and go for long, solitary walks which would give her the time to think ... she would not stay home and she would not fly south and become embroiled in the hectic gaiety of a beach resort. Her chin jutting stubbornly, she decided to add to her suitcase a pair of pure wool slacks and her white fur mittens.

She was kept busy most of the morning doing the last-minute things that were necessary if she was to leave the house for three or four weeks. She was trying very hard not to think about Patrick, but she was not wholly succeeding, for his image was constantly at the back of her mind, nagging her. She had not seen him for well over a week. Once she left the house she would not see him for four more. And when she came back, he would have vanished into the backwoods of New Brunswick. If he had not bothered to keep in touch with her the past few days, he certainly would not bother over the weeks and months of spring and summer. Whatever had been between them was over before it had really begun.

At eleven o'clock Moira picked up the rented car, a sporty and very comfortable little compact that was immaculately clean and responded to the controls like a well-trained horse with a touch of spirit. She had planned to drive straight home with it and load her cases; instead she found herself proceeding to Patrick's apartment block. After parking by the kerb, she scrabbled in her handbag for a piece of paper and a pen, and then wrote hurriedly, *Gone to New England for a month's holiday. Sorry not to have heard from you. Moira.*

Sorry was an inadequate word, but it was all he was going to get; she had swallowed enough of her pride in coming here as it was. Damned if she was going to swallow the rest and tell him how dreadfully she had missed him. She creased the note in half, hurried into the building and searched for Patrick's mail box along the row of locked metal doors.

'Can I help you, madam?'

Without turning around, she recognised the voice. She said distantly, 'I'm looking for Patrick Casey's mail box.'

'Down one row and six to your right, madam.'

She shoved the folded note through the slot. It seemed to meet opposition and she knew instinctively that the box was full of mail because Patrick had not yet returned. For a moment she stared blankly at the smooth sheen of the metal. Maybe something *had* happened to him. Maybe he'd had a terrible accident . . . maybe he was dead.

'Is there anything else I can do for you, madam?'

Find Patrick. Bring him home to me. She turned, said coldly, 'No, thank you,' and walked through the revolving door with all the disdain she could muster. No one would have guessed, looking at her, that her pride was in shreds and her heart full of terror.

She drove home very carefully, for there were patches of ice on the streets and the visibility was poor. By the time she had reversed her car as near to her front door as possible, reason had reasserted itself. If Patrick had had an accident, she would have heard about it on the news or read it in the papers. His was a household name in the city; the media could not afford to ignore such as he. Which was cold comfort, for it left her with the inevitable corollary that he was alive and well and not interested enough in Moira Tennant to pick up the telephone and call her.

She ate lunch, left a key with a neighbour, and loaded her bags into the car. It was snowing harder. The sensible thing would have been to delay her plans for another day: having waited eight years for a holiday, one more day was unlikely to make much difference. But Moira did not feel like being sensible. She wanted to flee from the city as quickly as she could, and to put as many miles as possible between her and Manhattan before she stopped for the night. She could not have explained this to anyone else; she only knew that it was so.

She made a last-minute check of the house and gave herself a cursory glance in the mirror. She was wearing a slim-fitting navy gabardine coat with a red silk scarf tucked into the neckline. Her hair was fastened in a knot on the top of her head; high black boots protected her feet. She looked chic and competent; only the clouded grey eyes that looked back at her from the mirror gave away her inner confusion. She pulled a face at herself, dragged on her long leather gloves, and ran downstairs. Swinging her handbag over her shoulder, she locked the front door behind her.

CHAPTER SEVEN

MOIRA headed north along Franklin Roosevelt Drive. The traffic was heavy, and the snow seemed to have affected everyone's mood for the worse. Horns blared. Cars whipped in and out of the lanes. A taxi driver shook his fist at Moira when she braked too slowly to let him in ahead of her. By the time she reached the toll stations for the Triborough Bridge, her nerves were stretched taut. She paid the dollar-fifty toll and came out of the gate, knowing she needed to bear left to head for New England. The route was clearly marked. She slipped into second gear.

To her right a long black limousine burst out of the gate, travelling much too fast. Moira saw it skid on a patch of ice and swerve towards her, and a fraction of a second before anything happened knew with a fatalistic certainty that the limousine was going to hit her. She swung the wheel to avoid it, but she was too late. The strident scream of metal and the jar of impact came as one. The little car was thrown sideways. Brakes screeching, a yellow cab coming up from behind missed her by inches.

Her ears were singing, her gloved hands gripping the steering wheel as if they were glued to it. Her cheek hurt where it had struck the side window. Vaguely she became aware that the car had stalled. It seemed to take immense effort to loose her hold from the wheel and turn off the ignition.

The door was wrenched open. A man thrust his face into the opening and began yelling at her. He had an accent . . . Italian? She listened, fascinated, certain that his eyes were going to pop out of his head. 'What the hell you think you doing? You make my passenger miss his plane. I shall sue! You hear me? I shall sue!

Goddamn women drivers. Never should let a woman behind the wheel. Never! You hear me?'

He was, quite literally, spitting with rage. His hair was as black as his eyes, and very greasy; he must have to shave at least twice a day, she decided detachedly. Very carefully she drew in a long breath and let it out again, then flexed her arms and legs one at a time. Everything appeared to work. She was not dead. That much was certain. She did not even appear to be hurt. In the rear view mirror, which was tilted at a crazy angle, she saw that her cheek was scarlet where it had hit the glass but that her hair-do was still intact. *Good for you, Moira*, she thought ironically.

'Why don't you say something? You think I'm fooling. I tell you, lady, I'm not fooling. My passenger miss his plane—it's all your fault!'

She brought her head around, looked the chauffeur straight in the eye and said clearly, 'Shut up.' Ignoring his sputtered obscenity—even though it was in a language she did not recognise, she was sure it was an obscenity—she edged her boots to the ground. He had, perforce, to move back. Grabbing the door for support, she pulled herself upright.

The two toll booths behind them had been closed. The traffic swirled around them, the other drivers too impatient to reach their destinations to bother about a minor accident. A uniformed bridge commissionaire was walking towards them. He looked so large and calm and competent that she was not surprised to find his voice as soothing as the rest of him. He said impartially to both of them, 'If you would just wait here, please. The police will be along shortly.'

'My passenger must catch his plane——'

'I'm sorry, sir, your passenger will have to wait for the police. Are you all right, ma'am?'

She gave him a weak smile. 'Yes. I'm fine.'

His brow puckered. 'I've seen you on television, haven't I?'

She knew he was making conversation to give her

time to gather her wits, and was grateful to him. 'I expect so. I advertise toothpaste and shampoo and cosmetics.'

'And some very expensive perfume. The wife always says she'd buy it if she thought it would make her look like you.' He turned his head at the sound of a siren. 'Here come the police. They'll require a statement from both of you. We'll have to get tow trucks by the look of things.' He sounded blessedly matter-of-fact.

There were two policemen, one young and bored, the other older and bored. The commissionaire walked away, his duty done. The chauffeur started a loud, voluble tirade of self-justification, scurrying behind the police officers waving his arms as they walked around the two damaged vehicles. Feeling very much *de trop*, Moira leaned her unbruised cheek on the top of the door and closed her eyes.

A car drew up in a shudder of brakes. A door slammed. A man's voice exclaimed, 'Moira! Darling Moira—are you all right?'

She looked up, knowing whom she was going to see, yet scarcely able to believe her eyes. 'Patrick?' she faltered.

He pulled her away from the door, put his arms around her and hugged her to him. 'You're not hurt?'

'N-no.'

'I was terrified when I recognised you standing by the car. You're *sure* you're not hurt?'

'My cheek's bruised, that's all.'

He took her chin in one hand and tilted her face. 'So it is. That'll be purple by tomorrow. Nothing else?'

There was so much solicitude in his voice, so much anxiety in the deep blue eyes ... and it was all an act. Moira pulled her chin free, stood up straight and decided quite rationally to lose her temper. She was due for it—and so was he. Adrenalin flooded her veins. She said sweetly, 'You're overdoing it, darling Patrick.'

'Overdoing it? Like hell. When I saw you'd been in an accident, I——'

'Yes, overdoing it.' Her voice rose. 'You're wasting your time writing plays. You should be acting in them.'

'What the devil are you——'

'You're a fake!' she stormed. 'A blue-eyed, gorgeous-looking fake. Other women might fall for your act. Your darling this and darling that and your incredible sincerity and your provocative remarks. But I'm not one of them! As far as I'm concerned you can go straight to hell and stay there—you'll be in good company. And on the way you can spare me all this touching concern about whether or not I'm hurt. You don't give a damn whether I'm hurt or not!'

'You listen to me, Moira Tennant! It took ten years off my life when I came through that toll booth and saw you'd been in an accident. If anything had happened to you——'

'—you'd have been devastated. Inconsolable. I'm sure you'd have fled straight to one of your actresses for comfort,' she hissed. 'In fact, why don't you do that anyway? Turn your car around and go back to Manhattan, Patrick—and leave me alone. You're good at that. You've been practising for the last ten days, haven't you?'

He lowered his voice from a shout to something approaching normality. 'I have to apologise for that.'

'Oh, please don't bother.' Her voice dripped with sarcasm. 'Just because I was naive enough to believe you when you said you'd phone, and foolish enough to be worried when you didn't, doesn't mean you have to apologise.' Her control snapped. 'How *dare* you do that? How dare you tell me you'd be in touch with me, and then not bother to do anything about it? I thought you'd been killed, or were ill. I'm so stupid that I *worried* about you. *That* should give you a good laugh. The famous Moira Tennant staying home evening after evening in case you should phone—believe me, I'll never do that again. Not for you or anyone else. I *hate* you, Patrick Casey! I never want to see you again.' Dimly she became aware that tears were flooding her eyes and pouring down her cheeks.

'Excuse me, miss.'

She turned her head, glared at the policeman through a haze of tears, said distinctly, 'Go away,' then put her forehead on the door of the car and let the sobs erupt from her throat.

Someone, somewhere, was making a terrible noise. Crying as if she would never stop. Sobbing and wailing and incoherently trying to explain why it was all so terrible ... with the crack of a gunshot, something struck Moira's cheek. Gasping for breath, she opened her eyes and stared at the policeman, who was facing her with his palm still upraised. She heard Patrick roar, 'What the hell do you think you're doing?' and saw him lunge for the policeman with murder in his eyes.

Blindly she thrust herself between them. Patrick's forearm struck her in the chest so that she fell back against the policeman with most of the breath knocked from her lungs. With what was left she quavered, 'Patrick—behave yourself! You can't go hitting policemen, they don't like it.'

Patrick looked very large, totally furious, and not in the mood to listen to reason. 'He hit you——'

'So did you. Anyway, I was hysterical.' She felt laughter that was not far from hysteria bubble in her throat again and swallowed hard; she did not think Patrick would appreciate her starting to laugh right now. And deep down, beneath the laughter, a very primitive part of her nature was gratified that he had sprung so fiercely to her defence. 'I'm okay now—I won't do it again.'

Reluctantly Patrick lowered his fists. The policeman gave him a baleful look and said coldly to Moira, 'Full name, please. And I need your driver's licence and vehicle permit.'

The rental agency will love me for this. She bent down and retrieved her handbag from the car, gave the policeman her licence then rummaged in the glove compartment for the other documents he required. In a carefully neutral voice she gave her account of what had happened.

The older policeman, the chauffeur, and a courtly, silver-haired gentleman in an overcoat whose label Moira would have recognised and respected anywhere, had joined them. The chauffeur seemed subdued, although the look he gave her was far from conciliatory. The silver-haired gentleman said with exquisite courtesy, raising Moira's gloved hand to his lips, 'I would have missed ten planes for the privilege of meeting the most beautiful woman in New York.'

It was impossible not to respond to such charm. 'Why, thank you,' she said cordially. She knew she must look far from her best, dishevelled, bruised, and tear-streaked. But if the silver-haired gentleman could ignore such details, so could she.

'Even more beautiful, if that is possible, in the flesh than on the screen. My name, by the way, is Randolph Eldridge III, from Newport, Rhode Island.' Still firmly holding her hand, he glanced up at Patrick, his faded blue eyes twinkling. 'Patrick Casey, I believe?' he added with gentle irony. 'What an exciting afternoon I'm having. Two celebrities in one accident.' He glanced beyond Patrick's shoulder. 'Ah, here comes the other limousine to take me to the airport. I must go. Miss Tennant, a pleasure to have met you. Mr Casey, I strongly advise you to bring your full creative talents to your apology and explanation . . . you wouldn't want to lose her, would you?' He raised his hat, then walked through the slush towards the waiting limousine.

Said Moira, warmly, 'I don't want a creative explanation. I want the truth.'

Disregarding her, Patrick announced peevishly, 'If I hadn't been here Randolph Eldridge III would probably have carted you off to Newport with him.'

Again she felt that ridiculous bubble of laughter in her chest. 'Jealous, Patrick?'

'Bloody right.'

With somewhat overdone politeness the younger

policeman said, 'You're free to go now, miss. I'd advise you to contact the rental agency as soon as possible. The tow trucks are on their way now.'

She gave him her best smile, wondering what he would tell his friends about the way the beautiful model Moira Tennant comported herself at the scene of a car accident, and said with equal politeness, 'Thank you very much. You've been very helpful.' She fluttered her lashes at Patrick. 'May I get a drive home with you, Mr Casey?'

'I should damn well hope so,' Patrick growled. But there was a spark in his blue eyes that made more than her lashes flutter.

They retrieved her cases from the battered little compact and put them in the boot of Patrick's car. As Moira got in, she remarked, 'I didn't think you owned a car in New York.'

'I don't. This belongs to the guy who lives next door to me. I borrowed it as soon as I got back and saw your note.' He started the car and added, 'That young pipsqueak of a policeman would love to catch me making an illegal U-turn. I'll have to go to the nearest exit and come back.'

Staring down at her gloved hands, Moira said quietly, 'Why didn't you phone me, Patrick? You promised you would.'

'Because I didn't have your phone number, Moira. It's unlisted, and every single operator in Manhattan is immune to bribery, blandishments or threats.'

'You didn't *have* it?' She gaped at him, her brain whirling. 'I never gave it to you?'

'Never. I never had to phone you, we always made our arrangements when we were together.'

'That's right,' she whispered. 'We did. Oh, Patrick . . .'

'I called the modelling agency. They wouldn't give it to me—behaved as if I was some kind of a sex maniac or a potential white slaver. I tried to call Ted Price, but he was away. I even called the hotel where you stayed in

Phoenix; at least they were polite in their refusal. I didn't know Anton's last name, and I couldn't remember Derek's. Oh, it was all great fun.'

Of all the reasons she had thought of, one so simple had never occurred to her. She said in a small voice, 'Couldn't you have written?'

'Same story. I know the location of your house. But I never noticed the name of the street, or the number. Told you I was absent-minded. All I could do was hope and pray you wouldn't cut me off your list. I had no idea you were planning a holiday. When I got home today after lunch, I found your note in my mailbox, read it and tore over to your house. But you'd just gone, so your neighbour told me, the one with whom you'd left the key. I figured you'd be taking Route 95 north, so I headed for the Triborough Bridge as fast as I could. And there you were.'

'Yelling at you,' she said apologetically. 'Oh, dear.'

'I'm glad you yelled at me. Shows you cared enough to be angry.'

'I was disappointed,' she said hastily. 'That's all.'

He gave her a sardonic sideways look. 'Yeah? I like my explanation better. Where were you going for your holiday, Moira?'

'I was planning to find a country inn somewhere in New England and plunk myself in front of the fireplace.'

'Alone?'

'Alone.'

'I ought to leave for New Brunswick in the next day or so. You could change your plans and come with me.'

'Oh, could I? Who says?'

'I do.' He took a hand from the wheel and rested it on hers. 'Please, Moira. I nearly went out of my mind stuck there in Ontario not able to reach you. I was lonely, I was jealous, I was afraid you'd have vanished by the time I got back—and you very nearly had. I don't want to leave you again.'

She was determined not to give in too easily. 'What if

I hadn't been planning a holiday? What would you have done then?'

'I'd have stayed in New York long enough to get some kind of commitment from you.' He gave her a crooked smile. 'Believe me, I've never delayed the starting of a play for any other woman.'

'I should be flattered, hmm?' she said drily.

'What's the matter? Don't you want to go to New Brunswick?'

'I—I'm not sure. You see, I lost all my trust in you these last few days. You'd said you'd phone and you didn't, so I didn't know what to believe. It was—upsetting.'

They were back on the bridge again, the wipers swishing back and forth to clear the windshield of snow. 'So now you're not quite ready to trust me again?'

'That's right.' Although not quite ready to trust herself might have been a more accurate statement.

'I'll wait, then. For as long as I have to.'

'Why, Patrick? *Why?*'

'Because I haven't any choice. I discovered that in Ontario. Kit, by the way, was in far worse shape than I'd expected. That's why I stayed so long.'

It was a relief to talk about Kit rather than about Moira and Patrick. 'Is her son all right?'

'Yes, he was fine. He got a bad scare, but I don't think there'll be any serious after effects. But Kit was ready to fall apart. Coming so soon after Sandy's death, Peter's accident was too much for her. She couldn't sleep, and if she did get to sleep, she had nightmares. She'd start crying and couldn't stop. She'd fly off the handle with the boys at the slightest little thing ... I was glad I was there, because I could take a lot of the pressure off.'

'Was she better when you left?'

'She had certainly calmed down. But Sandy's birthday is in a couple of weeks, and I know she's dreading that. One of the reasons I'm anxious to get to

New Brunswick is so I can invite her for a visit, it'd do her good to get away from home for a while. The boys love the place. I don't mean to put pressure on you by saying that, but it is a factor.'

'Does she date, or does she feel it's too soon?'

'Too soon. In fact, when I suggested it, she nearly bit my head off. I wish she would go out more, if only to take her mind off the boys and the house. A boyfriend from high school days who's newly divorced lives down the street—I'm sure he'd like to date Kit. Or even just be able to drop in and help her out with some of the chores. But she seems to think that would be disloyal to Sandy.'

They were back on FDR Drive. Moira murmured, 'Maybe you could drop me off at the car rental agency. It's on Second Avenue. I'd better go and face the music.'

'I've got an appointment with my agent in half an hour. But why don't we meet for dinner at seven-thirty?'

'Is there as little in your refrigerator as there is in mine?'

'That's the only reason I'm asking you out ... Will you give me an answer then, Moira?'

'Yes. Yes, I will.'

They agreed on a restaurant, Moira fixed her make-up, and Patrick let her off outside the rental offices. Resolutely she stepped inside.

Patrick was waiting for Moira outside the restaurant, his coat collar turned up against the wet snow. She got out of the cab and gave him a tentative smile. He drew her under the shelter of the awning, put his arms around her and kissed her. In one kiss he managed to combine tenderness, generosity and a devouring passion; she was incapable of rational thought by the time he released her, although she did know that her own hunger had been as blatantly revealed as his. She said shakily, 'I'm ten minutes late.'

'Worth waiting for. Will you go to New Brunswick with me, Moira?'

'After a kiss like that, how could I refuse?' Despite the lightness of her reply, the eyes she raised to his were troubled. 'Patrick, I have to say this. If we go, we sleep in separate rooms. I'm not agreeing to an affair with you.'

His eyes narrowed. 'Playing hard to get?'

'Saying it the way it is. The image I project is not necessarily the true one—you might be surprised to learn how staid my lifestyle actually is.'

'After the way you kissed me a minute ago, I might not believe you.'

'Oh,' she said recklessly—and truthfully, 'my response to you is unique.'

'Do you say that to all of them?'

'Perhaps you'll have to figure that out for yourself,' she retorted.

'Separate bedrooms . . . if that's what it takes to get you on that plane, then I'll go along with it.'

'You wouldn't . . . you won't . . .?' Her voice died away.

'No,' he said wryly, 'I wouldn't. You won't have to lock your door at night, Moira.'

In a rush, before she could change her mind, she said, 'Then I'll go.'

Perhaps she had expected him to sweep her into his arms again and give her another of those devastating kisses. Instead he said prosaically, 'Good. I'll call my travel agent from the restaurant and get him to make the arrangements as soon as possible. We mustn't waste any of your holiday.' He pulled open the door and ushered her inside, and for the rest of the evening devoted himself to being a charming and considerate companion.

CHAPTER EIGHT

LESS than twenty-four hours later Patrick and Moira were in an aircraft taxiing along the runway at La Guardia, bound for Montreal. From the perfection of Moira's appearance as she boarded the plane no one would have guessed what an unsettling mixture of bravado and trepidation was churning away inside her. Along with Patrick, everyone else no doubt assumed that a woman as sophisticated and chic as Moira Tennant thought nothing of an illicit holiday with a male companion. She knew better, and yesterday had done her best to inform Patrick. She would have preferred him to believe her, although she could understand why he had not.

Her cloak was camelhair lined in black and her sheath dress a stark combination of the two colours, while her accessories, including a wide-brimmed hat, were also black. Hat and cloak went in the overhead compartment; she settled in her window seat and buckled the seat belt. The aircraft was not large, so there were only her and Patrick on this side of the aisle. He smiled at her and said calmly, 'As we're going away together, I think it's time you told me more about yourself. You know, minor details like when you were born and where, whether you have any brothers and sisters, why you never talk about your childhood or your parents. Don't you agree?'

'Not necessarily,' she said coolly.

'Come off it, Moira. Do you realise I don't even know how old you are?'

'Thirty-three.'

'Your make-up's not that good. How about twenty-five?'

'Twenty-six.' Knowing she could not escape, she went

92

on rapidly, 'Born in Cape Breton, father coal miner, mother housewife, two older brothers who both work in the mines, several dozen aunts, uncles, and cousins. Graduated from high school, went to New York at age of eighteen. Will that do?'

'As a précis, it's fine. Not for some details. Are your parents still alive?' She nodded. 'How long since you've seen them?'

She hesitated. 'Two years.' She forestalled his next question by adding with a touch of desperation, 'I don't fit in there any more, Patrick. That's why I don't go. I've become a stranger in the house where I grew up.'

'Do you keep in touch with them?'

'I write to my mother every week. I used to phone, but Mum gets tongue-tied on the telephone and Da's too deaf. His hearing was damaged in a mine explosion years ago.'

'Is your mother as beautiful as you?'

'She might have been once. But too many years of hard work and worry and not enough money have aged her. I send her money every month, but instead of using it for herself she buys presents for her grandchildren and nieces and nephews. Oh, she might buy herself a pretty apron or a new set of bowls for the kitchen. But she still uses the old wringer washer in the scullery and hangs her clothes out on the line to dry.'

'Maybe it makes her happy to give to others.'

'Do you know what the trouble is?' Moira did not wait for an answer. 'She's in awe of me! My own mother waits on me hand and foot as if I'm a guest rather than her only daughter.'

'Do you go there dressed as you are now?'

Moira looked down at the simple lines of her dress and her plain leather boots. 'There's nothing fancy about these clothes.'

'Who are you kidding? You look expensive, exclusive, and untouchable,' Patrick said with brutal candour. 'I'm not surprised she doesn't know how to reach you.'

'Is this the first fight of our trip?' Moira demanded. 'I can always change my mind in Montreal—I don't have to go away with you.'

'What about your father? Is he the reason you left home?'

Not for the first time Moira decided Patrick was far too shrewd. 'Da wanted me to marry the boy next door. I was enough in fear of my father to run rather than risk confronting him. We never saw eye to eye on anything.'

'Was it your father you were running from, or the place?'

'Both, I suppose. It was so ugly there, Patrick. At least I thought so. Row on row of company houses. Black-grimed trees—everyone burns coal, you see. Even the birds looked dirty. Worse than that was the aura of hopelessness, because it's a dying industry, and the constant, unspoken anxiety. Accidents happen in mines, everyone knows that. Men die trapped thousands of feet under the sea. Oh, I hated it all so much! I grew up knowing I had to get out of there, that somehow I had to create for myself a life of beauty and order—where I had control.'

'Do you feel you've succeeded?'

'Yes,' she said stoutly. 'By looking at me you'd never know where I come from, would you?'

Patrick said soberly, 'Cutting yourself off from your roots is a dangerous thing to do. You *are* a coal miner's daughter, whether you like it or not.'

'I even changed my name,' she admitted. 'I grew up as Maura MacLeod. But that didn't have the right ring for New York, so I became Moira Tennant. Da didn't like that. But then he never understood why I had to leave in the first place. He hated what he called my fancy ideas. He thought I was a snob. Too good for Scots Bay . . . I didn't think I was too good for them! I just knew I couldn't live that way. I didn't want to marry the boy next door and have three or four kids who'd play in the slag heaps and always have to worry whether their father would come home from the next shift. I wanted something different for my children than that.'

'So you want to have children?'

She glanced over at him, dropped her eyes from the intensity in his, and mumbled, 'Someday, yes.'

'You do realise that sooner or later you'll have to make your peace with your parents and with the place where you grew up?'

Was that motive somehow imbedded in her blind drive to go north for her holiday? Intuitively Moira sensed that it might be, and that part of her disenchantment with her life in New York might spring from a self-imposed estrangement from parents and home.

The steward had wheeled the trolley for bar service to their seat. Moira ordered a rum and orange and firmly changed the subject.

They made their connections at Montreal's Dorval Airport with no trouble, and disembarked in Moncton after dark to find a foot of snow on the ground. 'There'll be more in the hills,' Patrick remarked. 'There always is.' He scanned the parking lot, located a four-wheel-drive Toyota land cruiser, and led her towards it. 'Friends of mine drove this in yesterday; they'll have opened the house up for us as well.' He put their cases in the back and unlocked the doors. 'All set?'

It was a business-like vehicle, built high off the ground. Moira clambered in, pulling the folds of her cloak around her, for the temperature was below freezing. Patrick started the engine, scraped off the windshield, and turned on the fan. The blast of cold air made her wish that her hat was less stylish and more practical: ear flaps wouldn't hurt. Patrick seemed to be immune to the cold. Whistling between his teeth, he drove out of the parking lot.

His property was thirty miles from the city of Moncton. After crossing the river, Patrick headed west. They wound up hills where the road was lined with spruce trees, and descended into valleys where brooks were still coated with ice and the bridges were built for one lane of traffic. Twice they saw the gleam of yellow eyes beside the ditches and Patrick said laconically, 'Deer. In spring when the snow's still deep in the woods they come out to feed in the open.' The snowbanks edging the road grew deeper; the houses were fewer in number and more widely separated.

Moira sat quietly, wondering what she had let herself in for. It was all far wilder and more isolated than she had anticipated; she had the frightening sense of leaving behind everything that was familiar to her and heading into unknown territory. With a virtual stranger, she thought, giving Patrick a quick glance. He did not look the slightest bit concerned about the blackness of the night or the paucity of houses; on the contrary, he looked relaxed, confident, and supremely happy. She said in a small voice, 'Do you have any neighbours?'

'Jessie and Dave live a mile from me—they're the ones who will have opened up the house. Old Fred Wallace lives a mile away in the other direction. He keeps me supplied with wood, and ploughs up the garden every spring.'

'Nobody nearer?'

'No. This is the country, Moira, not New York.'

Which was a redundant statement if ever she heard one. She subsided into silence again. The paved road turned into a dirt road, treacherous with ice. Eventually they turned off the highway, crossed a tiny bridge, and drove along a narrow lane towards a single light that beckoned to them from the side of a hill. Patrick's house was built of cedar and stone in a very modern design, the rooflines at varying angles, the windows and verandah orientated to the south, the chimney of rough-hewn granite. Patrick pulled up beside it, turned off the motor and got out. Slowly Moira followed suit.

The silence was absolute, for there was no wind, no traffic, no other humans beside themselves. Her ears rang with the quiet, so much so that she took a quick

breath to reassure herself that she had not suddenly
gone deaf. The snow lay deep and clean on the hillside.
The trees were as black as the sky; the stars seemed
close enough that she could reach up and pluck them.
They were also incredibly bright; those she was used to
in the skies over New York were but pale imitations.

She found herself watching Patrick. As he slowly
scanned his surroundings he looked like a man who has
come home after too long an absence; he had totally
forgotten her, she was sure. For him the awesome
silence and the black hills that loomed behind them
were familiar and welcoming. They posed no threat to
him, aroused no fear.

She shivered, for the cold was biting through her thin
leather gloves and elegant unlined boots. She said
loudly, 'I hope the heat's turned on.'

'What? Oh, the heat . . . Jessie will have turned it on.'

He resented being disturbed, she could tell. 'May I
have the keys? You can commune with nature if you
like, but I'm cold.'

He gave himself a shake. 'Sorry, Moira. There's
something about this place that gets to me. You have
no idea how good it feels to be back here.'

No idea at all.

Patrick unlocked the boot and passed her one of her
cases, taking the heavier one himself. They crunched
across the snow to the front door, Patrick unlocked it,
and they stepped inside. Moira's first impression was
one of warmth, her second as Patrick switched on the
lights, of space, for the house was constructed in an
open plan with cathedral ceilings and floors at different
levels. As Patrick led her to her room, the hallway
became a balcony overlooking the sunken living room,
which had a stone fireplace stretching from floor to
ceiling. The bedroom which was to be hers was
decorated in warmth earth tones. It had books on the
shelves, paintings on the wall, and plants at the
window, a far cry from the austerity of Patrick's New
York apartment. Suddenly feeling very tired, Moira

said abruptly, 'I think I'll go straight to bed.' But was it tiredness? Or was it an unhappy combination of homesickness and loneliness?

'Can I get you anything to eat or drink?'

'No, thanks.'

'I'll probably go for a walk, then. I may take the snowshoes and go up the hill to the maple grove. Sleep well.'

He was so obviously anxious to be rid of her, she thought crossly, as she watched him leave the room and close the door behind him. It was a new experience for her to have the outdoors as a rival; so much for her private worry that she might have to lock him out of her bedroom.

For a few minutes she stood still, hearing him moving around the house. Then a door banged shut and she knew he had gone. Letting out her breath in a little sigh, she took off her cloak and hung it in the wardrobe, and began to unpack. The task soothed her. When she had finished she had a bath, leaving her hair and make-up to the last. But as she put on a very elegant satin and lace négligé the colour of café-au-lait, she found herself conscious of the silence again. She must have been busy for nearly an hour—was Patrick still out? She glanced at herself in the mirror. The négligé covered her completely, and with her hair still piled on her head and her make-up on, she looked suitably aloof. No harm in checking to see if he was back.

He was not. She prowled around the house, absently admiring the plant-filled solarium in the kitchen, the lofty dining room and the workmanlike study, until the chiming of the grandfather clock in the hall told her he had been gone for an hour and a quarter. It was twelve-thirty, pitch black outside and very cold. He surely wouldn't stay outside by choice. No one in his right mind would. He must have had an accident. Or maybe he was lost.

She felt panic close her throat. What should she do?

The nearest neighbour was a mile away, she was not sure she could drive the land cruiser even if she found the keys, and she had no idea where to look for Patrick. Wringing her hands, she went to stand by the window, staring out into the impenetrable darkness. She'd give him fifteen more minutes. If he wasn't back by then, she'd get dressed and go looking for him.

Twelve of the fifteen minutes had crept by when she saw a black figure emerge from the woods and tramp down the hill towards the house. For a moment she was terrified, for its silent, purposeful approach held all the menace of her childhood nightmares. Then reason reasserted itself. It was Patrick, on snowshoes. He was safe.

When he came in the door she was still standing by the sink, her eyes huge, her hands clasped in front of her. He said sharply, 'What's the matter?'

'Why were you so long? I thought you were lost.'

'Lost—*here*? Darling Moira, I'd have to be blind to get lost around here.' He struggled out of his sheepskin jacket and threw his knitted toque on the counter. His cheeks were red with cold.

'Don't patronise me! I was worried.'

'Then you'd better learn something right now. I go for walks at all odd hours in the day or night and sometimes I'm gone much longer than I was tonight. You'll have an ulcer if you let yourself get in such a state every time I leave you alone.'

To her overstretched nerves there was contempt in his voice. 'I beg your pardon!' she flared. 'I'll make sure it doesn't happen again. And now I'm going to bed.'

But he had walked over to her, his eyes glittering dangerously as he caught her by the arm. 'Do you sleep with all that stuff on your face?'

'What's that got to do with you?' Moira retorted childishly.

'Well, tonight you're not going to.' He turned on the tap in the sink and reached for a cloth. 'Tonight I'm going to see what you really look like.'

'Don't you touch me!'

He was wringing out the cloth with one hand. 'You're in Pleasantvale now, not New York. I don't want a model in my house—I want the real woman.'

She kicked out at him with her bare feet. 'I'm no less real because I wear make-up,' she panted.

'When you hide behind it, you are. Hold still.'

She ducked, but he had caught her around the waist and was scrubbing at her face with the cloth. When she tried to scratch him he struck down her hand, and his heavy sweater protected his body. Wriggling and squirming, she sputtered out her entire stock of profanity and did her level best to damage his shins with her bare feet.

When Patrick had finished the job to his satisfaction, he put down the cloth, pulled the pins from her hair and allowed it to fall down her back. Then he took her by the shoulders, marched her down the hall, and stood her in front of the full-length mirror in his bedroom. 'Look at yourself,' he said roughly. 'You've never looked more beautiful than you do now.'

She saw a woman whose grey-green eyes were brilliant with rage, whose cheeks were flushed and whose honey-coloured hair framed a face vivid with life. 'You enjoyed that, didn't you?' she spat. 'Well, let me tell you——'

'I certainly did. But there's one thing I neglected.' As he brought her round to face him, his mouth found hers. His hands were wandering over her body, tracing the curve of her spine, caressing the swell of her hips and buttocks, finding the softness of her breasts. She felt the thrust of his tongue and the hardening of his groin and could have died from the bittersweet surge of longing that swept aside her anger as if it had never existed.

Then he had released her, again turning her to face the mirror so that her back was against his chest. His voice was not as steady this time. 'Now look at yourself.'

But Moira could not focus only on herself. She saw instead a couple: a glowing pliant creature in shimmering satin in the embrace of a tall black-haired man whose eyes were dark with desire and whose hands were even now smoothing the woman's body through the folds of her gown. Was that woman herself?

She watched the black head bend, felt the man's hands lift the weight of her hair and his lips slide down her throat. She closed her eyes, bringing her arms up to clasp his head and finger the silken thickness of his hair. His hands moved to cup her breasts, taut from her upheld arms. A shudder rippled through her frame. It was for this man that she had been born . . . it was for him that she had been waiting all her life.

Against her throat Patrick murmured, 'If we keep this up, you're going to have to lock your door.'

As slowly as if she had been drugged, Moira opened her eyes. Like a statue of two lovers the couple was still there, the man's hands at the woman's breasts, her hair spread across his chest. But the image in the mirror was not a statue. It was two real people of flesh and blood, whose flesh ached for each other and whose blood pounded in their veins. She had only to whisper, 'I've changed my mind,' and Patrick would carry her to the big bed and make love to her. The choice was hers.

She had hesitated too long. He muttered, 'Separate bedrooms, that was the agreement.' He lifted his hands from her waist and moved away from her.

She said uncertainly, 'No pressure? No force?'

'Neither one.' He ran his fingers through his hair. 'It's one thing to wash your face somewhat forcibly—— '

'Somewhat!'

'—because I want to see what's under all the powder and paint, but it's another to take you forcibly into my bed.' Deliberately he shattered the mood between them by giving her a brotherly pat on the behind. 'Go to bed. I'll see you in the morning.'

She could have stayed and argued. But she felt her feet carry her to the door. 'Good night, Patrick.'

'Good night.'

She did not lock her door, she knew there was no need. But it took her a long time to get to sleep, because her body throbbed with newly awakened needs and the image of the couple in the mirror had burned itself into her brain.

CHAPTER NINE

MOIRA awoke to a raucous chorus of crows, and sunlight streaming across her bed. She knew instantly where she was, and could not have quelled the uprush of happiness at the prospect of the days and weeks ahead to be spent in Patrick's company. She would not always wake up alone in her own bed. Sooner or later what had been started last night in front of the mirror would reach its natural conclusion, and she would awaken in Patrick's bed, his arms around her. Although she was willing to wait until the time was right, she was already beginning to hope it would be soon.

A light tap came at her door, loud enough for her to hear if she were awake, not loud enough to disturb her if she were still sleeping. 'Come in,' she called.

Patrick pushed open the door. He was carrying a tray with a small teapot and a cup and saucer on it. 'Time you were up. The sun's shining.'

She smiled at him, drinking in every detail of his appearance from the dark hair curling at the neckline of his shirt to his lean hips in tight-fitting jeans. 'You're spoiling me.'

'I have the feeling that for all your money and fame, you haven't been spoiled very much—am I right?'

'I suppose you are.'

'Have you ever lived with anyone, Moira?'

'His question took her by surprise. 'No. Never.'

'So I'll be the first.'

'Patrick, I——'

He put down the tray, leaned over her, and kissed her sleep-soft lips. Impelled by forces stronger than reason, she pulled him down on top of her. But he was heavier than she had expected; she gasped for air and suddenly they were laughing. Patrick nuzzled his face into her

103

neck. 'It's a line I'd never get away with in a play, but my first thought when I woke up this morning was of you.'

'Mine, too. Of you, I mean,' she murmured incoherently. 'But that doesn't mean I'm going to live with you. Stop that, Patrick—the tea's getting cold.'

He looked straight into her eyes. 'You know I want to make love to you, don't you?'

'Yes.' She was blushing again, but it didn't seem to matter. 'I woke up knowing that we would.'

He grinned at her, his teeth very white. 'The beast in me wants to do it right now—you're so soft and warm and beautiful. But my more civilised tendencies say to wait a while until we know each other better. I don't want us to rush into something that we might regret. I want it to be right for both of us.'

With her finger she traced the jut of his cheekbone, the roughness of his unshaven chin, the sensitive line of his mouth, and felt him tremble at her touch. 'So do I, Patrick . . . oh, so do I.'

He kissed her without passion, as if sealing a pact. 'I'll go and start breakfast. Are you hungry?'

Moira chuckled. 'For more than breakfast.'

'Shameless hussy. Breakfast is all you're getting.'

'The service around here is terrible,' she mocked, looking up at him through her lashes.

'Complaining already, huh? That's what happens when you invite a woman into your house.'

She was not sure she wanted to know the answer, yet had to ask the question. 'Have you invited women here before?'

Unconsciously he paralleled her own answer earlier. 'No. Never.'

'Oh. That's good,' she said with such transparent relief that he laughed.

'You're the first one—so you'd better behave. Breakfast in fifteen minutes.'

As he left the room, Moira found herself smiling idiotically at the closed door. Patrick Casey could make her angrier than anyone she had ever known, ignite her body as no one had before, make her laugh and make her cry. All of which was very far from boredom.

To top it all off, she thought exultantly as she jumped out of bed and turned on the shower, she didn't have to go to work for four whole weeks. She was a long way from New York with all the demands of photographers and agents and the necessity of preserving her image as a top model. Here she could be—despite what Margarita said—plain Moira Tennant. Or perhaps, she decided thoughtfully, even plainer Maura MacLeod.

They ate grapefruit and eggs Benedict and drank deliciously hot Java coffee at the pine table in the solarium, which was bathed in the gentle warmth of the spring sun. 'It's ideal maple syrup weather,' Patrick commented. 'Sub-zero at night, above freezing in the day.'

'I thought maple syrup came from Vermont?'

'Better maple syrup comes from the hill behind the house,' he boasted. 'Are you game to climb the mountain with me, and we'll tap a few trees? We could boil off the sap tomorrow and the next day.'

'Sure,' she said with the promptness of ignorance.

'I'd better come clean and say that once I've started work I won't be able to spend very much time with you, Moira. But for the next couple of days I can show you around, and tonight we're invited to Jessie and Dave's for dinner, so you'll meet them. You'll be free to take the Toyota anytime you want.'

'I'll be fine. I'm already feeling as though I'm on holiday.' It was true. All the alienation and loneliness she had felt the night before had vanished in the daylight. She was simply happy to be with Patrick in the place that he loved.

They cleared away the dishes, then Moira went to her room and pulled a sweater on over her shirt and tucked the hems of her jeans into long woollen socks that Patrick had loaned her. She bundled her hair under a woollen cap, added a windbreaker and mittens and went out to the back porch to try on Kit's high-laced moccasins. Fortunately they fitted. Patrick showed her how to do up the bindings on the snowshoes, and they set off up the hill.

In the clear morning light the setting of Patrick's home was spectacular. The house was perched halfway up the hillside, overlooking a valley of open meadows where a brook meandered through banks of alders; the valley was surrounded by rounded, tree-clad hills that were possessed of an immense dignity. Or were until Patrick yelled his name across the glen, and the hills threw it back in a garbled echo. She called her own name. 'Moira-ra-ra,' the hills called back.

It took Moira several minutes to get into the rhythm of using the snowshoes; she followed Patrick along a winding trail between the trees, secretly admiring the easy swing of his hips, already sensing that he was as at home in these woods as he was in the house below. The trail climbed steadily. Moira, who liked to think she was very fit, was panting by the time they stopped for a drink in a tiny brook that burbled between ice-coated rocks. She wiped her lips. 'Nothing that good comes out of the New York taps. Are we nearly there?'

'Just about.'

The evergreens thinned out, to be replaced by a tall stand of grey-trunked maples whose crowns sighed in the wind. Patrick pointed out the sugar shack, which was built of weathered lumber with a vent in its sloping roof. Inside were stacks of firewood, a metal stove, a large boiling pan and the sap buckets.

The procedure was simple. Patrick drilled a hole in the trunk, hammered in a plastic spout and hung on it a metal bucket with a hinged lid; a clear watery liquid began dripping into the bucket almost immediately. 'The sap's rising in the trees,' he explained. 'It has a measurable sugar content. When you boil it down, you're left with maple syrup, or maple sugar if you boil it longer. It tastes heavenly.'

Working side by side they tapped thirty trees. 'We'll

have to be up here early tomorrow,' Patrick added. 'It takes all day to boil the sap down.'

Moira was beginning to harbour the suspicion that a great deal of work was involved. 'How early?'

'Not before daylight.

She gathered up a mittenful of snow and lobbed it at him. 'How early?'

'Chickening out?'

'Answer the question, Patrick.'

'The earlier we start, the sooner we'll be finished. You don't want to be up here at midnight, do you?'

'I have the feeling I've been recruited as slave labour.'

'Now you're getting the idea.'

The trek back to the house was far less arduous. After lunch Moira curled up in an armchair in the living room with a book while Patrick worked in his study. Mid-afternoon he took her for another walk, this time to a tiny valley east of the house. He had cautioned her to be as quiet as possible. She saw why as they approached a clearing in the trees, for two deer were drinking at the stream. Their coats were dun-coloured, their legs delicate and attenuated, casting blue shadows on the snow.

The nearer one raised its head, looking straight at Moira with liquid brown eyes. Its white tail flashed a signal. In a series of graceful leaps the two deer vanished into the bushes on the far side of the stream.

Slowly Moira walked out into the clearing. The tracks of sharp-pointed hooves dented the snow: the deer had been real, not a vision or a dream. She said wonderingly, 'I can't really believe I'm here. I cannot imagine a world more different than the one from which I've come.'

Patrick was eyeing her narrowly. 'Don't get all dewy-eyed about the place. The deer are hunted every fall, some of them wounded and left to die by careless hunters. More of them starve every winter if the snow gets too deep. If you're by yourself in the woods and you have an accident, there aren't any pedestrians who'll see that you get to hospital—out here, you're on your own. You and your skills and strength pitted against an uncaring nature. Ruinous lumbering practices, acid rain, budworm spray—we've got them all.'

'If you get hurt in New York, the odds of being helped by a pedestrian aren't great,' she rejoined, frowning at him. 'There are problems everywhere you go in the world. But that doesn't mean I can't enjoy this place. The blue of the sky, the beauty of the deer, all the colours in the snow . . .'

'I thought you were in danger of romanticising the wilderness. I'm probably over-reacting, Moira, because I so badly want you to like it here.'

'How could I help it?' she said lightly. 'No coal dust on the snow.'

'No theatres or restaurants or opera houses, either.'

'No smog, no taxi cabs, no muggings on the street.'

'No streets.'

'Right!' She wrinkled her nose at him. 'Let's go home and build a snowman, it's years since I've done that.' How easy it was to say 'home'. Yet although this was home to Patrick, how could it be for her? She needed the city for her livelihood as much as he needed the hills and valley for his.

The snowman was an artistic masterpiece, flaunting a vermilion toque and scarf, his round face smiling impartially at house, valley, and his two creators. Moira patted snow around his nose to give it an exaggerated hook. 'There,' she said complacently. 'Now he looks like you.'

'He does, does he?' Patrick picked up a handful of snow and advanced on her. 'Tell me I'm better-looking.'

She gazed raptly at the snowman's dumpy figure. 'He's much more handsome than you.'

Patrick made a dive for her, she dodged, and the snowball hit the snowman's protruding belly. Giggling, she flung some snow in Patrick's direction, which by pure luck hit him on the collar of his parka, melting against his neck. With a roar of outrage he was after her. She ran up the hill, hampered by the deep snowbanks, felt him cannon into her, and landed flat on her back. As he dribbled wet snow down her neck, she shrieked with helpless laughter, her cheeks pink, her hair falling all over her face. 'You're the handsomest man in the world!' she choked. 'Devastating. Irresistible. Gorgeous.'

'That's better,' he growled. 'Just so long as you appreciate me.' Then he was kissing her, his lips cold and wet.

Water was trickling down Moira's neck. Her jeans were damp and her mittens soaked. None of it seemed to matter. Against his mouth she murmured, 'I've had such fun today, Patrick.'

'So have I . . . I already feel as if you belong here. I'm sorry if I was abrupt with you when we arrived last night, Moira. I was so afraid that you'd hate it here.'

She was suddenly frightened by the intensity in his eyes. 'I don't hate it at all. But I am getting decidedly damp.'

'I'm rushing you again, aren't I? In New York you always seemed so poised and aloof—unreachable. When I look at you now, I can hardly believe I'm lucky enough to be holding you in my arms.'

But New York is my home. Involuntarily she shivered, her eyes clouding. She already knew how closely attuned he was to her moods and emotions; when he saw her reaction his jaw hardened and his touch was carefully impersonal as he hauled her to her feet. 'You'd better have a hot bath. I told Jessie we'd get there about seven.'

Moira was ready a few minutes early. She was wearing a full-length tweed skirt in muted shades of blue and mauve, with a plain silk blouse and a crocheted shawl; she had applied a minimum of make-up and had left her hair to fall straight down her neck. She hoped she was not overdressed; for all she knew, the unknown Jessie might be wearing jeans. To have to worry about her choice of clothes was a new sensation.

She was reassured when she saw Patrick, for his slacks and dark blazer seemed to complement her own outfit. And Jessie, who was a tall vivacious redhead, was wearing a full-length skirt with a cashmere sweater. She and her husband Dave were unaffectedly happy to see Patrick again, and made Moira feel genuinely welcome. Dave, lean and prematurely grey, had been a chartered accountant in Montreal, while Jessie had been a guidance counsellor. Four years ago they had quit their jobs, sold their house, and moved with their two children to Pleasantvale. Dave was now a sheep farmer and Jessie a teacher in the nearest elementary school; they were very happy with their choice. 'We always make sure we keep enough money aside that we can take a trip to Montreal or Toronto,' Jessie explained. 'We go to plays, the symphony, and shop like mad— and then after five or six days we're ready to come back here to the peace and quiet. For us, life is simple here. More time for the things that matter.'

'Don't you ever feel isolated?' Moira ventured, and sensed Patrick's stiffening to attention.

Dave answered her. 'We work at keeping in touch. We have subscriptions to *The Glove and Mail* and *The New York Times*, we have a fortune in cassettes and records, and Jessie has such an uncontrollable lust for books that we're never short of anything to read.'

'If we were, we'd just go up to Patrick's,' Jessie supplied. 'We cultivate our friendships here, Moira— you need a sense of community, especially in winter.' She smiled at her husband. 'In Montreal we always seemed to be fighting the clock and the traffic. Tearing here and there. We're both so much more relaxed here.'

Out of the corner of her eye Moira could see that Patrick, too, had relaxed; his friends had given the answer he had wanted her to hear. *It's not that simple*, she wanted to cry. *I have to earn my living. I can't do that in Pleasantvale.*

The talk drifted to the achievements of the Montreal Symphony. The meal was tasty and the conversation stimulating, and Moira thoroughly enjoyed herself. As they drank their coffee, she regaled them with a selection of anecdotes from her modelling career that ranged from the humorous to the disastrous, then Patrick described the 'Man For All Seasons' studio sessions down to the last styrofoam snowflake. They lingered around the fireplace with their liqueurs. It was past midnight when Patrick and Moira drove home across the bridge and up the narrow little lane.

'I had a wonderful evening,' Moira said warmly. 'I really like your friends.'

'I enjoyed myself as well.' He glanced at his watch as he parked the Toyota. 'I'd better set the alarm for tomorrow morning.'

Moira was too full of wine and good food to relish the thought. Yawning, she gathered up her skirt and walked to the house. In the kitchen she smiled sleepily at Patrick. 'Good night. You'll wake me in the morning?'

'Yes.' He was still hunched in his sheepskin jacket, his eyes sombre; she felt the first touch of unease. 'This probably isn't the time or the place, but I'm going to say it anyway. You know I'm in love with you, don't you, Moira?'

She wrapped her arms around her body. 'I've wondered.'

'No need to wonder any longer. I love you and I want to marry you.'

As a young girl dreaming of escape from the town where she had been born, Moira had sometimes imagined a man saying these words to her, and her own ecstatic response. The reality was far different. 'It's too soon, Patrick. We scarcely know each other,' she blurted.

'I know all I need to know. You're ambitious and gutsy and hard-working—I knew all that before we left New York. And every day I'm discovering your warmth and passion.'

New discoveries for me as well. 'How can we fall in

love, though? It doesn't make sense. You live here and I live in New York. There's a world of difference between them—it's not just a matter of physical distance.'

'I earn more than enough to support us both.'

His voice was even and he was scrupulously keeping his distance from her. But he was fighting for her with all the force of his personality. Moira spread her hands helplessly. 'I've always worked, ever since I can remember. Part-time after school and on weekends and then in New York since I was eighteen. I couldn't give that up. Oh, I'm enjoying a few days off, it's wonderful to have a holiday. But after a while I'd be miserable without something to do. Besides, I like being independent and having my own money.'

He said stubbornly, 'I'm in New York for two or three months of every year, and you could surely take a couple of months off to come up here.'

'So are we married for four months and not for eight? It would never work, Patrick.'

'What am I supposed to do, then? Tell myself I'm no longer in love with you because it's not practical?' he said savagely.

'*I* don't know,' she wailed.

'Do you love me, Moira?'

It was the most difficult question he could have asked. Unconsciously her fingers tugged at the fringe on her shawl. 'I love being with you. You make me feel alive and happy. And—and I want to sleep with you. But does that mean I'm in love with you?'

'How would you feel if you were told you could never see me again?'

'Terrible,' she whispered.

'How would you feel if I told you I was married to someone else?'

She scowled at him. 'I'd kill her and ask questions afterwards.'

Some of the strain eased from his face. 'You look fierce enough to do it! Don't worry, you won't have to. You're the first woman I've ever wanted to marry, and

I knew it within ten seconds of seeing you. Don't ask me to explain, because I can't. But equally I can't let you disappear from my life.'

His words were battering her until she no longer knew what she believed. How easy it would be to fling her arms around his neck and cry *I love you*, and how wonderful a four-week honeymoon would be amid these lonely hills! But then what? He would stay here to write his play, she would go to New York to face photographers and television cameras, and, at night, an empty bed. She said raggedly, 'Patrick, I'm tired out and I don't have any answers.'

'The very qualities I admire in you are the ones that are coming between us,' he rasped. 'If you weren't ambitious and courageous, you wouldn't have got to the top. But now that you're there, you're not going to abandon that position for a mere man.'

'You're twisting my words—I'm not in love with my own importance! But I've worked hard to get where I am, and I don't know how to do anything else. Sure, you can say that all I do is wear expensive clothes and look beautiful, and believe me, there are times when I'm bored to death with it. But I'd be worse off doing nothing. I don't work just because of the money. I work because it makes me feel useful, part of society, independent, capable of looking after myself, all sorts of reasons.' She rubbed at her eyes. 'Oh, damn. I didn't mean to start a sermon on the work ethic. Please, Patrick, can't we continue this in the morning?'

'What else is there to say?' he responded bitterly. 'You've said it all. I should never have started this in the first place. Go to bed, Moira, and forget I ever said anything.'

She had no need to tell him how impossible that would be. Her instinct was to go up to him and put her arms around him, soothing the tension and anger from his face. Grimly she held her ground. 'Good night,' she said stiffly. 'Don't forget to wake me in the morning.' *Marvellous exit line, Moira. Maybe you should be the one writing plays.*

Her bedroom looked warm and inviting. It seemed a lifetime since she had woken up that morning wanting Patrick beside her in the bed. *He's spoiled it all*, she thought wretchedly. *How are we ever going to live in the same house for the next four weeks?*

CHAPTER TEN

MOIRA felt as though she had only just gone to sleep when Patrick knocked on her door without opening it and called, 'Time to get up, Moira. Breakfast in ten minutes.'

No cup of tea in bed this morning. Certainly no kiss. She sat up, wishing maple syrup had never been invented, and staggered into the bathroom, regarding her bleary-eyed reflection without enthusiasm. A shower helped. Afterwards she dressed in the most workmanlike clothes she could find and pulled her hair into a ruthlessly tight braid. In New York she would have spent half an hour making her face presentable to the world. This morning she did not even bother with lip gloss. If it was the real Moira Tennant he wanted, let him have her in all her glory.

Patrick was polite, friendly on the surface, and a million miles away. Much farther away than the distance between New York and Pleasantvale, Moira thought miserably, agreeing with him that yes, it was a lovely day and thank you, she would have coffee. She was not surprised when he said at the end of an artifically sustained conversation about the dinner at Jessie's, 'I'm going to take my notebook with me today. I've started jotting things down for this next play, and there's lots of time with nothing much to do up at the shack.'

'Maybe I should take something to read,' she said pleasantly.

'You don't have to stay up there all day if you don't want to.'

Just how was she supposed to interpret that? 'I'll see how it goes,' she responded, giving him a meaningless smile.

They made a picnic lunch and snowshoed to the shack. Patrick lit the fire in the stove while Moira started emptying the sap buckets into a larger pail. The sap looked exactly like water; she hoped Patrick knew what he was doing. She soon discovered that it was hard work lugging the big pails of liquid from tree to tree on snowshoes; inevitably some of the camaraderie resurfaced between her and Patrick. Together they strained the sap and poured it into the flat metal pan that sat on top of the wood stove. 'Now we wait,' said Patrick. 'All we have to do is keep the fire stoked.'

It took a long time for the sap to come to a boil. But eventually clouds of steam were curling upwards to escape from the vent in the ceiling, and the temperature in the shack climbed steadily. Moira took her turn at shoving the hardwood logs into the door of the stove, wincing from the heat and the glowing orange coals. Her fingernails were soon broken and dirty; it was a good thing Derek couldn't see her now, she thought, pushing a strand of hair back from her sweating forehead. But the sap was gradually thickening and turning to a pale gold.

Patrick spent a good part of the day sitting on a stump with his notebook on his knee. Moira did not object to this, for she felt they both needed time to forget some of the things that had been said the night before. She read her book, brought in more wood from outdoors and stacked it neatly, inspected the rising level of sap in the buckets on the trees, and watched the shadows of the maples lengthen on the snow. Despite what had happened last night, she discovered that she was happy spending the day with Patrick in an old wooden shack in a grove of trees. The tension and boredom that had been so much a part of her life in New York had vanished overnight; the most important consideration on her mind was the slowly increasing temperature of the syrup as the steam evaporated. The temperature was all-important, Patrick had said.

There was a flurry of activity at the end, for the pan had to be hauled off the stove, the syrup filtered and poured into sterile jars, and the jars capped. They ended up with half-a-dozen bottles of clear golden liquid. 'It's worth its weight in gold,' Patrick commented wryly. 'All that work for six jars.' He had saved a little syrup at the end, which he boiled a few minutes longer then poured on the snow to harden; it made a sweet chewy toffee. 'Heavenly!' Moira said happily, licking her sticky fingers one by one. 'No doubt dreadfully fattening, but who cares? Now what do we do?'

'Clean up, and carry the filter and the jars down the mountain. It's going to be dark before long.'

Moira was aching in every muscle when they reached the house. They lined up the six precious jars on the counter and regarded them with satisfaction. 'Want to do it again tomorrow?' Patrick asked.

She gave a mock groan. 'Ask me when I've had a shower.'

'Making maple syrup is one way of separating the men from the boys,' he teased. 'If we go tomorrow, then Dave will collect the sap the next couple of days. The season's nearly over.'

He was rinsing out the felt filter in the sink, and she found herself watching the play of muscles in his forearms. 'Patrick,' she said impulsively. As he glanced at her, smiling, her heart did a sudden, and disturbing, flip-flop in her breast. 'I just want you to know how happy I am to be here. With you, I mean. Can you simply accept that at face value? Please don't rush me like you did last night.'

He turned off the tap, rubbed his hands down his jeans, and took her face in his palms. 'My beautiful, scruffy, and far-from-clean Moira,' he said gently. 'I blew it last night. I lay awake half the night telling myself what an idiot I'd been, that I lay awake the other half wanting you . . . you blush entrancingly and you've got dirt on your nose. I don't think you'd pass muster as a model in Pleasantvale let alone New York.'

'You sometimes have trouble with my professional image, don't you?' she said carefully.

'Yes. Not because I'm threatened that you're independent and successful—please believe me when I say that. More because the passionate, laughing creature I love seems to get lost under layers of paint and lacquer.'

'I *was* in danger of losing her, you're right. There's something about you that brings her out, though.'

'I'll try and be content with that for now.' He bent over and kissed her, taking his time, then muttered, 'Who am I fooling? I want all of you, body and soul, right now. Patience never was one of my virtues.'

'I'm beginning to realise that.' She stood very still, remembering the sensual imprinting of his mouth on hers, knowing it would take very little for them to tear off each other's clothes and make love on the kitchen floor.

But then Patrick moved back. 'Go to bed, woman, before I forget all my good intentions.'

So she did.

The next day the sap yielded nine jars of syrup, and it was late evening by the time Patrick and Moira got home. Fortunately there was some leftover stew which Patrick re-heated. After she had eaten, Moira headed for the bath tub and bed, sleeping the clock round. In the morning Patrick had left her a note on the kitchen table saying he would be working all day, so she pottered around the house making a dessert, washing her clothes, and reading. On Patrick's shelves she found a novel set in a Nova Scotian coal-mining town; reading it was like re-reading the script of her own life. The cadence of the narrative became the cadence of her father's voice, while the characters were like some of the people she had lived with for eighteen years. Memories came flooding back: her father sitting on the front step in a clean white T-shirt drinking cold beer, his eyes black-rimmed with coal dust; her mother's inarticulate, pathetic terror the day of the explosion in the colliery, her equally silent tears of joy when she found out her

husband was safe. Malcolm and Mairi MacLeod . . .
they had brought up their three children on strict
Calvinistic principles, where hard work was a virtue and
too much pleasure a sin. Malcolm occasionally bent
those principles: witness the beer; but Mairi never did.
Little wonder Mairi regarded her only daughter
askance, as if she had hatched an exotic bird of paradise
instead of the expected dusky sparrow.

That afternoon Moira went for a long solitary walk,
following the stream where she and Patrick had seen the
deer; for the first time in eight years she allowed the
memories of her childhood to surface naturally in her
mind, and found she could regard the unhappy, driven
Maura and her stern, unyielding parents with a level of
compassion and understanding that was new to her.
Her parents had done the best they could. They must
have been hurt and bewildered when their only
daughter had rejected them for a lifestyle that was
totally alien, and had even changed her name—the
ultimate symbol of rejection. Perhaps it was time she
went back to Scots Bay. But this time she wouldn't
wear her camelhair cloak and her designer dress. She'd
wear—she looked down at herself—blue jeans and a
windbreaker, and she'd take her mother a new set of
dish towels rather than a huge bouquet of flowers. In
other words, she thought, staring unseeingly at the
sparkling waters of the brook, she'd go back a Maura,
not Moira . . . With renewed energy she set off down
the hill.

When Jessie and Dave came for dinner that evening,
Dave was unmercifully teased for his yield of only five
jars of syrup. Patrick looked tired. Long after she was
in bed that night, Moira heard him prowling around the
house.

The days slipped by. On one level Moira was deeply
content, luxuriating in the lack of deadlines or
commitments and taking full advantage of the
opportunity to mentally assess the direction her life had
taken. She went for long walks. She visited Jessie and

Dave. She read, wrote letters, and listened to music. She relaxed.

On another level she was lonely. She saw little of Patrick, for he spent hours at a time in his study, the door firmly shut. From the little he said, she knew he was having difficulty getting the first scene off the ground. He had confessed tersely that starting a play was bloody awful, by far the most difficult part of the whole process. She helped the only way she could, by making sure he got regular meals and by keeping the house tidy and clean, a dual role whose traditional nature made her smile. Her mother would be proud of her.

However, as the days went by, some of Patrick's tension communicated itself to her. When she heard him leave the house at night to walk alone among the black spruce trees, she would lie awake until she heard him return; as she listened to him pace up and down in his study through the day, she longed to be able to help, yet lacked the courage to knock on his door and suggest that he take a break. She felt alienated from him, and useless; frustrated, and very much alone. As the tension mounted in her, a confrontation became more and more inevitable. The blow-up came the day he left the meals she had prepared for him untouched on the tray.

It had been a long day. Moira had woken to the drumming of rain on the roof and had opened her curtains on a dismal view of pewter-coloured clouds shoving their way between the mountains and dumping rain on hill and valley; soaking, purposeful rain that looked as if it could go on for ever. The snow was melting, exposing patches of bedraggled dead grass; rivulets of water raced down the hillside, scouring the rocks bare. The spruce trees were hunched in abject misery. A day, obviously, to stay indoors, for five minutes in the rain would saturate one to the skin. So much for her plan to go up the mountain and remove the buckets from the maple trees.

Patrick was locked in the study, Jessie was working, and Dave was away, and the rain had bared so much slick ice on the driveway that Moira was afraid to take the Toyota into town. She turned on the radio for company and all morning pottered around the kitchen, enjoying the appetising odours of chocolate chip cookies and a crabmeat casserole. At twelve-thirty she knocked on Patrick's door. 'Lunch is ready,' she called.

'Do you mind leaving it on a tray? I'm right in the middle of something.'

She did as he asked, although she would have much preferred his company. After she had eaten, she cleared up the kitchen, read for a while, religiously went through her exercise routine, and washed her hair. Two hours remained before she could decently start preparations for dinner; there was a limit to how much time she could spend in a kitchen. She stared out of the window at a view that had not changed appreciably since morning. The patches of grass were a bit larger. The spruce trees looked if anything more sodden and miserable. Nothing else had altered.

It rained in New York. But New York was filled with people and noise and ceaseless movement. Moira leaned her forehead on the cold pane, swept by a longing for pavement under her feet, a chorus of horns in her ear, the mushrooming of umbrellas on Fifth Avenue as the crowds jostled at the traffic lights. Heavy rain always seemed to cause traffic tie-ups. The cabbies would be bad-tempered, the pedestrians worse. Yet she would give almost anything right now to be yelled at by a cab driver or pushed into a puddle by a kerb-side crowd. When it rained in New York you could go to a movie or a concert, a restaurant or an art gallery, any one of a thousand department stores or boutiques. Everything was there. You had only to take advantage of it.

Her mind made a dizzying leap back to Patrick's proposal of marriage. For two months of the year he would be in New York. But for the other ten months? She could not live here for ten months with nothing to do. She would have to have a job or she would go crazy. But what could she do in Pleasantvale?

The rain dripped monotonously from the eaves as her thoughts carried her inexorably forward. She had never deceived herself about the longevity of her career. Most top models lasted five or six years and then were pushed aside in favour of newer, younger faces. The same would no doubt happen to her. But she had never worried about this. She had invested her money wisely, and when the time came she would buy into a restaurant or a boutique where her face and presence would lend a certain prestige. She could do that in New York. But—she pulled a wry face—she could not in Pleasantvale. The conclusion was inevitable. She could not marry Patrick. It would never work.

Her hands were cold. Her whole body was cold. *You cannot marry Patrick . . . it's impossible.*

But I want to, a voice screamed back, and dazedly she considered the implications of that instinctive denial. *I want to marry Patrick? Does that mean I love him?*

She did not know. She felt none of the certainty she had always assumed she would feel when she fell in love. She only knew that she was lonelier today in his house with him scarcely thirty feet away from her than she had ever been in her house in New York. And that the thought of losing him filled her with an inchoate, paralysing terror.

Dismal thoughts, as dreary as the unrelenting rain. Moira made herself a cup of tea, ate three of the chocolate chip cookies, and decided it would be a treat to see even Derek's joyless face. She must be in a bad way.

For dinner she roasted a loin of pork with potatoes and onions, serving it with apple sauce and broccoli. Dessert was a Bavarian cream which had turned out perfectly, a minor miracle, as she was an erratic cook. But when she called Patrick he told her in an abstracted voice to leave the tray outside his door, he'd get it in a minute. She bit back a variety of replies, none of which were polite, did as he asked, and ate a solitary meal in the living room in front of a blazing fire—that, at least, was cheerful. An hour later she went to pick up his tray. It was still sitting on the hall carpet, the gravy congealed, the potatoes dry, the broccoli looking and smelling as unappetising as only leftover broccoli can. She said with ominous calm, 'Patrick, you haven't eaten your dinner.'

Even through the closed door he sounded impatient. 'I'll get it in a minute.'

She thrust open the door without knocking and stepped over the offending tray. 'Don't bother. It's ruined now.'

'What on earth are you talking about? he said irritably. He was seated at his desk among a sea of papers, some scribbled on, some crumpled, some neatly typed.

'I left the tray outside your door an hour-and-a-half ago.' As her eyes wandered to the table by the window she gave a yelp of rage. 'You didn't eat your lunch either!'

'Stop fussing, Moira. Pass me one or the other of them and I'll eat something now.'

'I worked hard to make those meals appetising,' she stormed. 'You could have done me the courtesy of eating them while they were hot.'

'You sound horribly like our old housekeeper.'

'Little wonder when you act like an irresponsible child!'

He stood up, shoving his typewriter aside. 'So you want a fight, do you? Good! I could do with one right now. And no, Moira, I wouldn't advise you to throw that tray at me. The consequences could be very unpleasant.'

'Perhaps it would be worth it,' she said between gritted teeth.

He was giving the contents of the tray a leisurely survey. With deliberate provocation he remarked, 'I really had no idea you were so domesticated.'

As she snapped the tray down on the table, the water rocked back and forth in the glass; the crabmeat casserole stirred queasily. She said the one thing she should not have said. 'What else is there to do in this godforsaken place?'

His whole face closed, and instantly she regretted her words. He loved his house on the hillside. Her criticism was a rejection both of it and of him.

'So it's come to that already—after what, eight days? Do you miss New York, Moira?'

She stood very straight, the roast pork like a hard lump in her stomach. 'Today I did.'

'That does not augur well for my proposal of marriage.'

'Oh, do stop talking like a character in one of your plays,' she snapped.

His voice roughened. 'How can we get married if you can't even live here for eight days?'

She had asked herself the same question. 'Look at it from my point of view,' she said furiously. 'It's pouring rain, I'm cooped up in the house, and you haven't spoken ten words to me since the weekend.'

'I *told* you I'd be impossible to live with when I'm starting a play!'

'You certainly weren't exaggerating.'

'Put that bloody tray down and come here.'

A note in his voice warned her she might be wise to obey. She put the tray on the desk, edging aside some of the crumpled papers with exaggerated care. Then she walked over to him, her chin high, her eyes green rather than grey—a signal Margarita would have recognised. Making him a sweeping curtsey, not an easy gesture in jeans but one she accomplished with considerable flair, Moira said dulcetly, 'I am yours to command.'

'I bet,' he answered rudely. 'The day you obey me is the day I start to worry.'

'I could say the same of you,' she snorted. 'Patrick, didn't you even get hungry all day? You haven't eaten a thing since breakfast.'

'I wasn't aware of being hungry, no. A few threads and themes finally started to come together today, so I guess I was oblivious to the clock and the state of my stomach. I'm sorry, Moira—I can see you put a lot of effort into those meals.'

'It's okay.' The neglected meals were not really what they were fighting about.

As always, Patrick was quick to pick up his cue. 'You really don't like it here, do you?'

She hesitated, choosing her words with care, wanting to be absolutely truthful. 'I love the beauty and the silence of the valley. It's so peaceful. I like your house and your friends. But none of that is enough for me, Patrick. I don't have enough to do. If—if we were to marry, how could I ever find a job in Pleasantvale? It's not exactly the centre of the world.'

'It's not New York, is what you mean.'

'New York is where I have all my contacts and connections.'

Patrick gave her a kiss that was more abstracted than loverlike and said helplessly, 'What the devil are we going to do? We fight cat and dog, yet the thought of you getting on the next plane to New York terrifies me. *Terror*: a state of intense fear. That's what the dictionary says. And the dictionary's right.'

She remembered the cold smoothness of the glass against her forehead. 'I feel the same way.'

He was still holding her by the shoulders, although she was not sure he was aware of the contact. 'Don't catch that plane yet.'

'I won't.'

'We could re-heat the dinner in the oven, and then you can sit and watch me eat it.'

She smiled faintly. 'All right.'

And that is what they did. But inwardly Moira knew nothing had been solved, it had only been pushed out of sight.

CHAPTER ELEVEN

THE next day Moira made reservations to fly from Moncton to Sydney to visit her parents. While she knew she had to tell Patrick her plans, somehow the right opportunity did not present itself, for his routine of long hours in the study had resumed despite their last fight. Two days passed. The night before she was due to leave she still had not told him.

She had gone to bed early and had fallen asleep. She woke with a start, sitting up in bed with her heart racing in her chest. What had she heard? Had Patrick left the house for another of his nocturnal walks? She glanced at the bedside clock. It was one-thirty. She had been asleep for two-and-a-half hours.

She lay down and resolutely closed her eyes. When she opened them again it was one-thirty-six and she was more wide awake than she had been at eight o'clock the morning before. She got up and pulled on an old blue woollen housecoat that was a cast-off of Kit's; she had not worn the café-au-lait négligé since Patrick had scrubbed her face. In bare feet she padded into the hall.

Patrick was not in his bedroom, his study, or the kitchen. He must have gone out. She opened the refrigerator door and took out a container of milk, and was walking towards the cupboard for a glass when she stopped in mid-stride, her head poised. If Patrick was out, who had made that noise in the basement? Or had she imagined it?

Frozen to the spot, she waited. Then she heard it again, a dull thud as though something had been dropped to the ground. It was not the sort of noise the furnace made, or the pump, for she recognised those sounds now and had relegated them to the back of her awareness. No, it was something different.

Very quietly she put the milk on the counter and walked to the top of the stairs. There it was again . . . she tiptoed down the stairs, keeping close to the railing, and stood for a moment in the downstairs hall. The furnace room was at the end of the hall, the washer and dryer to her left along with a storage room. The noises were coming from behind a partially closed door to her right, a door she had never really noticed before; and they were undoubtedly of human origin.

A bar of light fell across the hall carpet from the room within. Greatly daring, she crept along it and poked her head around the door.

The room was a miniature gymnasium, complete with an exercise bicycle and some weight-lifting equipment. Patrick was standing in the middle of the carpet, his feet braced as he strained to raise a set of weights above shoulder-height. He was wearing a pair of grey running trousers laced low on his hips, and nothing else. His teeth were clenched, his forehead and chest slick with sweat. Fascinated, she watched the play of muscles across his torso as the bar went higher, higher. Then with a grunt he lowered it to the ground—the thud she had heard—and stood bowed over it, his breath rasping in his throat, his back heaving.

He had not seen her. She could leave and he would never know she had been there. Instead she deliberately moved the door so it squeaked on its hinges and said calmly, 'I thought you were a thief.'

He jumped and looked up. 'Moira! What are you doing down here?'

'I heard noises and didn't know what they were. So I came to investigate.'

He wiped his forehead with the back of his hand. 'And what would you have done if I'd been a thief?'

She grinned. 'Picked up the smallest weight and bopped you.'

'I don't doubt you would. I'm sorry I woke you.'

His chest was still rising and falling with the intensity of his breathing. She felt desire uncurl within her and said gently, 'You can't keep up this pace, Patrick. Working all day and then up half the night as well.'

'I made some progress today. Hopefully over the next two or three days, it'll fall into place. I hate to be acting so much like a tormented artist—but starting a play is always like this. I don't yet know the characters well enough to hear their voices clearly, yet I have to make them speak in order to get to know them. Vicious circle.'

He was trying to speak lightly, but his eyes were sunk deep in their sockets and the skin stretched tautly over his cheekbones. She dropped her gaze, seeing the dark hair that curled between his nipples and arrowed towards his navel. Because his trousers were of a lightweight knit fabric, she could have been in no doubt about his gender. Knowing exactly what she wanted, she walked up to him, rested her palms on his chest, and said, 'You haven't slept properly since we got here.'

He stirred restlessly. 'Don't worry about it, Moira.'

'It's partly because I'm here, isn't it?'

'I hoped you wouldn't guess that.'

His hands were hanging by his sides. She reached down, took one, and put it at her waist, then did the same with the other. Raising her face, she said, 'Kiss me—please?'

He dropped his hands from her hips as if the contact had scalded him and stepped back. 'Moira, *don't*! Why do you think I've stayed away from you the last few days? Because it's gone beyond the point where I can kiss you and walk away, that's why. I want to make love to you so badly that it's become an obsession. So for God's sake don't torment me like this.'

She gave him a rueful, and very loving, smile. 'You're going to make me say it, aren't you? Patrick, don't you understand? I want to make love to you, too. Now. Tonight.'

He searched her face with his eyes. 'You mean that?'

'Yes. If you want me.'

'*If* . . . God in heaven!' He swept her into his arms,

straining her to him as if he was afraid she might vanish. When he kissed her, it was with the hunger of a man who has been starving.

She was breathless and trembling when his lips moved from her mouth to her throat. His hands roughly pushed aside the collar of the old woollen robe. It was Moira who unbelted it and let it slip to the floor so that she was standing only in her nightgown, a simple pastel shift loose enough to hint at the body beneath without revealing it.

Patrick's hands stilled. He said hoarsely, 'You're sure, Moira?'

'Yes, I'm sure. I——'

But his lips silenced what she had been going to say. In a slow, sensual caress his palms moved the length of her body, learning the curves of waist and hips, moving upward to cover her breasts. Her heart was pounding. He must have felt it, must have sensed her surrender from the way her body arched towards him and from the moan of pleasure she gave as he teased her nipples.

Her whole body was flooded with an agony of desire. Her nails dug into the hard planes of his back, rippling down the long curve of his spine. He clasped her buttocks and drew her closer, so that she felt against her thigh the hard shaft that was all his need of her. His voice husky, he said, 'Let's go upstairs. I need a shower—I'm coated in sweat.' He left a trail of kisses down her shoulder. 'You can take one with me.' Gathering her into his arms, he picked her up and kicked the door open with his foot.

'I'm heavy,' she protested.

His laugh was as carefree and joyous as a young boy's. 'Why do you think I've been down here weight-lifting for the last week? So I can lift you effortlessly in my manly arms, of course. All heroes are supposed to be able to do that, aren't they?'

She rested her cheek against his hair-rough chest. 'I think you smell nice.'

'You *must* be in love. Believe me, I'll smell better for

a bit of soap and water.' He had carried her upstairs and down the hall to his bedroom. It had a stone fireplace and bookshelves and a very large bed; a door to the right led to a bathroom, decorated in grey and red. Patrick put her down, turned on the shower, and untied the cord at his waist, stepping out of his pants.

His body was lean and hard, infinitely beautiful. Overwhelmed by an unexpected, unnerving shyness, Moira whispered, 'If I take a shower, I'll get my hair wet.'

'We'll wrap a towel around it.' He reached for the skirt of her gown and lifted it over her head, then stood looking at her naked body so intently that her flesh was suffused with heat. He said finally, 'I'm the man supposed to be adept with words, yet all I can say is how beautiful you are and how much I love you.'

She had difficulty finding her voice. 'Perhaps that says all that needs to be said.'

'Yes . . . except that I want you. That needs to be said as well.'

He lifted her under the spray of hot water, which instantly doused his shoulders and streamed down his chest. Bending to kiss her, he said, 'We'll have to share the soap.'

She chuckled breathlessly. 'Now that's intimacy!'

'We'll do more intimate things than that before the night is done, darling Moira.'

Greatly daring, she took the soap from him and lathered the breadth of his shoulders and back, then, when he turned around, rubbed his chest in smooth strokes. All the time she did so, he was playing with her breasts, finally bending his wet head to kiss them, his lips encircling the swollen tips. 'Oh Patrick,' she moaned, 'I want you, too.'

Quickly he took the soap from her and washed the rest of his body, then turned off the water. The towels were thick and fluffy; he watched her every movement as she dried herself, smiling at her shyness. Before they left the bathroom, he rubbed the steam from the mirror, then pressed her body against his chest, wrapping his arms around her. 'Remember the last time we saw each other in the mirror? It seems an age ago.'

She saw the same couple, but this time they were naked, the woman's full breasts supported by the man's forearm, her smaller body only partially hiding his. She saw his lips move, heard him say against her throat, 'Come to bed with me, Moira,' and knew in her heart that the time was right.

In the bedroom Patrick pulled back the steel-grey spread and lifted her once again, laying her on her back on the sheet, then climbing in beside her. Not saying a word, he kissed her, his fingers moulding the arc of her collarbone. It was a kiss that seemed to last forever, his tongue exploring her lips and mouth even as his hands wandered even lower, from the soft weight of her breasts to the concavity of her belly and the silken smoothness of her legs. Every nerve in her body recorded the slow, sensual progress of his hands. Then with infinite sensitivity he parted her thighs and touched her where no one had ever touched her before.

Moira had never felt anything so total and all-encompassing, so much a blend of pain and pleasure. It was as though waves were tumbling on the beach one after the other, but faster and faster until in a great surge of power and a thunder of spray they fell on her and she was lost in the sun-touched dazzling white of foam and ancient waters. She heard herself cry out in mingled surprise and joy and opened her dazzled eyes to meet the unguarded tenderness in Patrick's. 'What did you do to me?' she whispered. 'Patrick, that was wonderful.'

'If I didn't know better, I'd almost think you've never done that before.' There was irony in his smile. 'It's been a while since you've had a lover, hasn't it, Moira?'

She put her arms around his neck, pulling him on top of her, glorying in his weight, in the breadth of his shoulders and the weight of his thighs. Opening her legs, she felt his body's instinctive thrust, felt fear and wonder and pride that he should want her so much, and said softly, 'I've never had a lover, Patrick. You're the first.'

She had often imagined herself telling him this, and had wondered how he would react. Perhaps deep within her she had been afraid that he would disbelieve her. Or worse, laugh in her face. Now she watched the play of expression in his face, saw incredulity change to a startled, joyful acceptance of her words. He said slowly, statement rather than question, 'You're a virgin.'

'Yes.'

Very gently he moved his lower body against hers. 'No one else has ever done this to you. Or this. Or this.'

Her body convulsed with pleasure, her eyes full of wonderment. 'No. Oh, no.'

Leaning on one elbow, he took her hand and guided it the length of his body. 'You've never touched a man this way before.'

On her face, clearly to be read, shyness was conquered by curiosity and a new, touching boldness. 'Never,' she whispered.

'Dearest Moira . . .'

'I'm glad you're the first,' she said fiercely.

'It wouldn't have changed my love for you if I hadn't been. But I'm glad, too.'

'You'll be gentle with me?'

'I wouldn't hurt you for the world. But, Moira—I don't understand. You have to be one of the most beautiful women in a city with any number of handsome and eligible men. I asked you once if you'd ever lived with anyone, because I couldn't bear not knowing, and you said no. I never felt you'd make love lightly or promiscuously, you didn't seem the type for one-night stands—but equally it never occurred to me that you'd never made love at all.'

Her hand, which had been stroking the interplay of bone and muscle in his shoulder, inadvertently caught in the slim gold chain around his neck. 'Who gave you that?' she said abruptly.

'My mother. It's a reproduction of an Aztec medallion. Reproduction because the original was pure gold, which you certainly couldn't wear on a chain around your neck.'

'Oh.'

'You thought it was another woman.'

'Yes.'

'My mother, I assure you. So you don't have to rip it off my neck and throw it to the floor. Or choke me with it.'

'I wouldn't do a thing like that.'

'Yes, you would. I'm glad it's not just me who gets jealous. Tell me why all those handsome men in New York never got near you, Moira.'

She settled herself more comfortably in the curve of his body. 'In Scots Bay I certainly wasn't going to make love to anyone. I'd seen too many of my friends get pregnant and have to get married. I wanted to get out of there too badly for that. My first year in New York I was too busy to have time or energy for a social life, and I soon discovered that in the modelling world one can make it to the top on one's own merits; it wasn't a question of whom one slept with. That was fine with me.' Her eyes clouded. 'Then when I was nearly twenty I met Mike. He was two years older than me, an artist. He'd graduated from art school and was living on an old frame house on Grove Street in Greenwich Village. He was young enough then to play the part of the artist. Beard, beret, paint-stained clothes. But he was just as ambitious as I was, and in the end that's what came between us.'

'Did you love him?'

'I was head over heels in love with him. Under the beard and the paint he was extremely good-looking, and he had all the brooding intensity and the passion that I felt a true artist should have. He wanted me to move in with him and be his model. Mind you, he wasn't above suggesting that I cook his meals as well.'

'And share his bed.'

'That, too.' She looked up at Patrick with some of the confusion of the younger Moira in her eyes. 'I wanted to, Patrick. I was a normal, healthy young woman with all the appetites of youth, and he was very persuasive. Whenever he sold a painting, which wasn't very often, he'd do something crazy like fill the room with scarlet roses, or give me a pair of cheap gypsy earrings in a box from Tiffany's. He'd strike up a conversation with anyone, he had massive self-confidence. You never knew quite what he might do next.' She sighed unconsciously.

'Let me guess,' Patrick supplied. 'You got the kind of offer at work that you'd been waiting for, and he didn't want you to do it.'

'I got a contract for catalogue work. It paid well, and it was the first step up the ladder. I *had* to take it. But Mike didn't see it that way. He was far too egotistical to share me. He wanted all of me or nothing. Either I lived with him and absorbed myself into his life—or I got nothing. That was the choice ... So I took the nothing. I signed the contract and I never saw him again. He went to Europe a couple of months later with a very beautiful young art student, had two children by her, left her, and now lives in Italy with a wealthy—and widowed—contessa. His art, they say, is derivative.' She grimaced. 'So much for Mike.'

'You were obviously hurt.'

'For a while I contemplated nunneries or a jump off the Brooklyn Bridge. But I didn't have time for either one. The catalogue work was very demanding, and then I got my first television audition and started to make a bit of money, and gradually I got over him. Still, I was in no hurry to fall in love again. And then, you see, as I got more and more successful and noticed and talked about, the telephone hardly ever stopped ringing and to all the handsome, eligible young men I said no thank you, I have a headache, or words to that effect, until the word got around that I was beautiful but unavailable.' She gave a derisive smile. 'Don't get the wrong idea, I

was never seriously tempted. But can you imagine if one
of my dates had discovered what you've discovered
tonight—I'd have been the laughing stock of the whole
crowd. It's a very closed world, the world I live in, and
virgins are far rarer than fine rubies.' She flicked the
medal on his chest. 'Or pure gold.'

Patrick grinned maliciously. 'You were hoist with
your own petard.'

'You don't have to look so pleased about it! Because
the truth is, Patrick Casey, that until I met you I was
perfectly content with my virginal status.'

He rested his cheek on her hair so that his face was
level with hers. 'Darling Moira, as we're into
confessions, you'd better tell me something else. Are
you in any way protected against the fate that overtook
the young girls in Scots Bay?'

She looked at him in consternation. 'Pregnancy, you
mean? No, I'm not.'

'I was afraid that was what you were going to say.
Assuming as I did that you were a woman of the world,
I also assumed that you would have taken—er,
precautions. I'm afraid, my love, you'll have to retain
your virginal status until we can get to town.' He must
have seen the blank disappointment in her face. 'We
can't risk a pregnancy, Moira. Our lives are complicated
enough as it is what with your job and mine, your
house in New York and mine here. I love you and I
want to marry you, which means I want you to bear my
children—but not now. Not yet.'

Moira looked less than convinced. 'I suppose you're
right.'

'We'll only have to wait until tomorrow,' he coaxed.
'Stop looking as though it's the end of the world.'

She said, wide-eyed, 'I've made reservations to go to
Scots Bay tomorrow.'

His voice was like a whiplash. 'But you're coming
back?'

'Of course—don't look like that, Patrick. Of course
I'll come back.'

'How long will you be gone?'

'A week at the most. It's time for me to go—or so I thought when I made the plane reservations. Right now it seems as though my timing's atrocious.'

'Celibacy's good for you, they say ... So you're returning to your roots?'

'I hope I'll find them.' She managed a smile. 'You'll be pleased to know I'll be wearing my blue jeans.'

'I'm glad you're going, Moira. I think you need to make your peace with your father and mother. You'll give me their phone number before you go? I'll call you during the week.'

She said with astonishment and delight, 'You will?'

'You'll get more words out of me long distance than you have living in the same house ... You don't quite believe in me yet, do you?'

'It's all happened so fast.'

'I'm real—cross my heart.'

She placed her hand against the wall of his chest in a gesture that was meant as a joke but was instantly transformed into something else, a flame of awareness, a searing need. She glanced down at their naked bodies lying side by side, and whispered, 'I know this is real.'

'All too real,' he groaned, throwing his thigh across her and drawing her close.

The next few minutes were filled with small, intimate discoveries that burgeoned into frantic excitement and the cruel knife-edge of frustration. Patrick flung himself off her to lie face down on the bed, his fists clenched, his breathing ragged. Helplessly Moira sat up, her knees bent under her, her hands kneading the knotted muscles at the base of his neck. 'Please, Patrick ...'

'We can't!' His voice was muffled in the pillow. 'We don't know what's happening between us yet, you're not even sure you love me. We can't risk starting a child.'

I don't care about the risk, she wanted to scream. *I want your weight on top of me, your body within me, your rhythms, mine ... how can you deny me?*

She was not even aware that she had spoken the question aloud until he grated, 'I'm denying myself as well.'

His features were rigid with tension. In genuine remorse she cried, 'Oh Patrick, I'm sorry—I should never have gone downstairs to find you. I've only made everything worse, haven't I? That wasn't my intention at all.' Suddenly she could no longer bear being in the same room with him, let alone the same bed. She scrambled to the floor with more haste than dignity and fled into the hall.

Patrick caught her at the doorway to her own room, grabbing at her shoulder and pulling her around so that he saw the tears pouring down her face and distraught, drowned eyes. 'Sweetheart, don't cry.' He drew her into his arms, holding her as he might have held a child. 'I'm glad you came to my room. We *will* make love, Moira—I promise you that. And I'll give you all the pleasure that I can.'

'You just have to touch me to do that,' she snuffled. 'I need a handkerchief.'

In her room he gave her a couple of tissues and found a nightdress in her drawer, which he slipped over her head. Her nose was red and her lashes wet, her shoulders drooping forlornly. He said matter-of-factly, 'I'll go and get a pair of pyjamas and then we'll sleep together.' She nodded without looking at him, and when he came back a few minutes later she was still standing in the same place. He said gently, 'Let's get into bed—you look worn out.'

Obediently she climbed into the bed, turning her back to him. He got in beside her, drawing her against his chest and holding her with an arm lying heavily across her breasts. In a small voice she said, 'Patrick, I'm frightened. I discovered something tonight—I'll never be able to make love to you and then get up the next morning and leave. As if nothing had happened. Never . . . Is it the same for you?'

'I'm afraid so.'

'I *have* to go back to New York. I've got contracts and appointments that I can't break.'

'All contracts come to an end. Don't fret, Moira. Go to Scots Bay tomorrow and when you come back we'll see what we can work out.'

He sounded very sure of himself and very comforting in the darkness. Moira did not see how a week in Scots Bay was going to change anything, but she was too tired to argue. With a tiny sigh she snuggled into the curve of his body and closed her eyes.

CHAPTER TWELVE

MOIRA woke first in the morning. The bedside clock said ten-thirty. She blinked and looked again, but the hands were in the same place and the clock was busily ticking. She should not be surprised. Heaven knows what time it had been when they had finally got to sleep last night. Or rather, this morning.

Beside her she heard Patrick's deep, even breathing. Turning her head very carefully so as not to disturb him, she let her eyes wander over his face. Although his eyes were still lined and he had a dark shadow of beard on his chin, he did look more rested, less strained, than he had yesterday. Many a model would have envied him the length and thickness of his lashes, she thought. Not to mention the raven-blackness of hair. Lying against her as he was, she could tell that even in sleep he was fully aroused. Half-smiling, half-blushing, she edged away from him.

His eyes flew open, for a fraction of a second blank with the transition from sleep to wakefulness. Then they smiled at her with such transparent love that he was beguiled. He said lazily, 'Good morning ... er, what did you say your name was?'

'We were in too much of a hurry last night to bother with introductions,' she said primly.

With an insouciance she could not have bettered, he asked, 'In too much of a hurry to do what?'

'To go to sleep, of course.'

'Of course,' he concurred gravely. 'Unfortunately if I stay here any longer I shall have matters other than sleep on my mind.'

'It's not your mind I'm worried about.'

Grinning, Patrick rolled away from her. 'Wise woman! I'm going to get rid of my frustrations by going outside to split some wood—it sounds as though the rain's stopped.'

'Shall I call you when breakfast's ready?'

He kissed her quickly. 'Best offer I've had this morning.'

'Oh, I can make you a better one.'

'I'm sure you could.' He laughed. 'I like my eggs well done.'

As Moira fired a pillow after him, he ran from the room and she was left standing by the bed with a foolish smile on her face and happiness lilting in her heart. Going to the window she opened the curtains on a sun-drenched morning that echoed her mood just as the hills had once echoed her name.

She showered, pulled her hair into a simple knot, and dressed in jeans, a plain shirt and a V-necked cherry-red pullover, tucking a toning silk scarf into the neckline of the shirt. She made the bed, her eyes smiling at a dozen little memories, then headed for the kitchen. From the window she could see the woodpile by the shed. Patrick, in his shirtsleeves, was rhythmically swinging the axe, splitting the birch and maple logs. She could hear the thunk of the axe as it hit the block, her eyes following the elegant arc of the blade through the air and the flowing practised movements of Patrick's body. Humming to herself, she took the bacon and eggs from the refrigerator and turned on the stove. Within a few minutes the kitchen was filled with the mingled odours of bacon and coffee, and a Vivaldi concerto was warbling away on the radio.

She did not notice that the regular blows of the axe had ceased. She was slicing bread for the toaster when the back door opened. She turned with a smile, a greeting on her lips, but the words froze in her heart. Dropping the knife with a clatter, she ran over to him. 'What happened?'

He was clutching a handkerchief to his cheek, the blood startlingly red against the white fabric. He said hastily, 'It's nothing serious. A chip flew up and struck me on the cheek. Can you take a look and see if I got it all out?'

She grabbed the nearest box of Kleenex and pulled out a chair. 'Sit down.'

When he took the handkerchief away from his face, the blood gushed down his cheek. She staunched it with a handful of tissues. 'I think it was a log, not a chip,' she said weakly. 'The cut's well over an inch long, and looks deep. You'll need stitches, Patrick. Where's the nearest doctor?'

'Thirty miles away. What time's your flight?'

'Two-forty, I think.'

'We'll just make one trip, then, once we've had breakfast and you've packed.'

His hands and voice were steady, but he was very pale, and the cut had not stopped bleeding. 'Don't you think we should go right away?'

'Don't worry, I'm not going to pass out.'

She sensed he would not change his mind. 'Where do you keep first-aid supplies?'

'Cupboard under the sink in my bathroom.'

Moira found a plastic box with a red cross on it, scrubbed her hands, and taped sterile dressings over the wound, trying not to hurt him, wincing inwardly when she saw him flinch. Then she made him a cup of hot, sweet tea. He ate very little. Moving as quickly as she could, she finished her own breakfast, cleaned up the kitchen, and went to her own room to pack.

Within fifteen minutes she was ready to leave. Patrick was still pale, and she suspected from the vertical lines between his brows that he had a headache. She said crisply, 'I'll drive.' Her suspicions were reinforced when he did not argue.

She drove fairly slowly, lacking a feel for the vehicle, which was unlike anything she'd ever driven before, and nervous of the patches of ice that yesterday's rain had bared. The land cruiser took hills, ice and ruts in its stride. Moira was feeling considerably more confident by the time they reached the outskirts of the city and

crossed the Petitcodiac River. Patrick directed her to
the general hospital where he had arranged to meet his
own physician in the emergency department.

Moira had had little experience of hospitals. The
receptionist filled out a form, took Patrick's medicare
number, and said briskly, 'Down the corridor, sir, third
door on your left. Dr Reynolds will find you there. You
can wait over there, madam.'

Said Moira, 'Let me go with you, Patrick?'

'Want to hold my hand?' he teased.

'I'd rather be with you,' she said stubbornly.

'Come on, then.' Ignoring the receptionist's dis-
approving eye, he led her down the corridor to the third
door on the left. The room was small, immaculately
clean, furnished with a narrow white bed, a couple of
stools, a sink, and an array of bottles and instruments
from which Moira averted her eyes. Dr Reynolds
breezed in, short, stocky and totally bald, and ripped
the dressing from Patrick's cheek. 'Hmm .. she took
the axe to you, did she?' He winked at Moira. 'How
long since you've had a tetanus shot, Pat?'

'I've no idea.'

'Better give you one. I'll have to freeze the area to
stitch it.' To Moira, 'Hold his hand, love. this'll hurt.'

She averted her eyes from the wicked-looking needle,
clenched Patrick's fingers and her teeth, and stared at
the opposite wall, feeling almost as though the needle
was being jabbed in her rather than in Patrick. *Maybe
this is why husbands have labour pains*, she thought
fuzzily. *I can't say I blame them*.

Dr Reynolds kept up a constant stream of
conversation, none of which Moira could recall
afterwards, and eventually Patrick was left with a neat
row of stitches in his cheek. 'There,' said the doctor
with professional satisfaction. 'Money-back guarantee
you won't be able to see where it happened in six
months' time.' He rummaged on the shelves and
dumped five or six white pills in a bottle. 'Take these if
the pain bothers you. Come back next week and

someone'll take the stitches out. Thursday or so.' He gave Moira an ebullient smile, said, 'Look after him,' and went out, whistling.

'I'm glad that's over,' Moira declared.

Patrick was putting on his jacket. 'I think you minded it more than I did.'

'I think so, too.'

'A sure sign you're in love with me, my darling.'

'I'd feel the same for anyone.'

He held out the hand she had been clutching. The marks of her nails were still indenting his skin. 'Really?' he drawled.

She blushed at the sight of the telltale marks, said crossly, 'Really,' and marched out of the room ahead of him.

They had a light lunch in a restaurant on Mountain Avenue, Patrick chewing with difficulty because of his frozen cheek, and then proceeded to the airport. It was a perfect day for flying. Moira heard herself say, 'I almost wish I weren't going now that this has happened. Are you sure you'll be all right?'

He kissed her, then muttered, 'My mouth feels funny—can't even kiss you properly. I'll be fine, Moira.'

They went inside, where Moira checked her baggage and bought a couple of magazines. Her flight was called. At the entrance to the security area she turned to face Patrick. *You're only leaving him for a week. Stop acting as though you're leaving him forever.*

I can't help it. I don't want to leave him at all.

You're hooked, Moira. You're in love.

Shut up and go away.

Uncertainly she said, 'Goodbye, Patrick. Take care of yourself, won't you?'

'I'll meet you here when you come back.'

Her smile broke through. 'I'd love that. No time zones to confuse you.'

He managed a very creditable kiss in spite of his frozen mouth. 'Don't fall for the boy next door.'

'Don't have any actresses in the house while I'm gone.'

'I love you, Moira.'

As always, he had the power to strike her to the heart. 'Oh, Patrick ... dear Patrick.' Standing on tiptoes, she gave him a soft, lingering kiss, then hurriedly turned away and entered the security area. When she and her handbag had been duly scanned, she looked back. He was still standing there, his blue eyes steady on her face. She blew him a kiss and hurried into the waiting area, wanting nothing more than to indulge in a hearty cry.

Moira was so used to air travel that she no longer paid much attention to the mechanics of it. She used the journey to Sydney to mentally change gears from Patrick to her parents. Each aroused confused emotions in her, although of a very different nature. Nor was she quite sure how to cope with either one. She took a cab from the airport into the town, seeing once again the flat countryside covered with scrub, the distant gleam of the sea, the scattered, heterogeneous houses. They passed the old brick high school, the church where she had attended a young people's group, and the black tower of the colliery where her father still worked. Little had changed. A few new houses had been built, a couple of stores had changed hands on the main street and a couple more had closed down, but otherwise all was as she had left it. But as the taxi turned into the street where her parents lived, Moira knew something had changed. Normally she found the drive from the airport to her home deeply depressing, for it would arouse all the old ambivalent feelings about the place where she had been born and raised. Today she did not feel that way. Her vision was less critical, her mind more ready to accept that she herself had sprung from this community of stubborn hard-working Scots who wrested a living from deep under the ground.

The cab drew up outside the door of a terraced

house, distinguished from its neighbours by an almost obsessive cleanliness. The path of crushed cinders was newly raked, the door had a coat of fresh green paint and the brass knocker shone. For the first time it occurred to Moira that while her own search for beauty had led her far away from this coal-mining town, her mother was able to find beauty in the simple, everyday objects around her: the gleam of brass, the sheen of a polished mirror, the exquisite order of her small domain.

She crunched up the pathway lugging her case, her grey eyes thoughtful. The same sense of order prevailed in the town house that overlooked the river in faraway New York, and was essential to Moira's peace of mind. There was undoubtedly more of Mairi in her then she had been willing to acknowledge.

Before she could lift the knocker, the door opened on well-oiled hinges. 'Hello, Mum,' said Moira.

Mairi MacLeod surveyed the tall slim figure in blue jeans and snow jacket, and gave a surprised smile. 'Well, now, Moira ... come in, dear, do. Your da doesn't dig enough coal for us to heat the outdoors.' She offered a lined cheek for a kiss, then stood back a little. 'You look different,' she said quizzically.

'I feel different, Mum. More like Maura and less like Moira.' Her mother, unlike her father, had called her by her new name for several years now.

Mairi had never been one to beat about the bush. 'How did that come about, now?' she said, hands on her hips.

Moira smiled at her affectionately. Mairi wore her grey-streaked hair pulled back into an uncompromising bun and had no time for make-up and such frivolities, but her bone structure was good and her eyes as clear a grey as a young girl's. 'I'm dying for a cup of tea,' Moira prevaricated. 'Then I'll tell you. Where's Da?'

'On the late shift. He'll be in at ten.' Mairi led the way down the narrow hall to the kitchen, which overlooked a tiny patch of grass, two black-limbed, disheartened poplars, and the back yards of another row of houses. The oil stove threw off a lively heat, the late afternoon light glinting on the chrome curlicues that bedecked its four, stout legs. Those curlicues were part of Moira's earliest memories; she had gazed at them in wonder as a baby crawling on Mairi's well-scrubbed linoleum. The table was pine, dented and chipped, each gouge a part of Moira's history. Here her eldest brother Alan had stabbed the table with the carving fork in a fit of rage; he had been soundly spanked, as she recalled. Here she herself had dug a series of numbers into the soft wooden surface one winter evening when she had been doing her homework. Patrick would like that table, she thought, wishing with a pang of longing that he were here.

Her mother had filled the kettle and set it on top of the stove. 'I made oatcakes,' she said.

It was like Mairi to offer only her cheek to be kissed but to have spent the morning baking her daugher's favourite cookies. 'Even though I've got your recipe, mine are never as good as yours,' Moira rejoined. 'Let's slather them with butter and jam.' To hell with her twenty-three inch waist, she thought recklessly, although she would never have used the word hell in front of her mother.

'You look younger, somehow,' Mairi supplied. 'Softer. Prettier. Are you still doing that modelling?'

'I'm taking a few days off right now. But yes, I'm still doing it.' Her mother had put a plate of oatcakes on the table. Moira began buttering them; it seemed a long time since she and Patrick had eaten lunch. 'I really needed a holiday. I'm not enjoying the work nearly as much as I used to, but I can't come up with a substitute.'

'No doubt you've been working too hard. You always were a worker, Moira.'

Moira glanced around the spotless kitchen. 'I come by that honestly, Mum ... But you're right, I've been working hard. For eight years, you might as well say.

Driving myself so I'd get to the top. And now I'm there and it's not as marvellous as I thought it'd be.' Her mouth twisted. 'In fact, if you want the truth, I'm bored to tears.'

Mairi measured a generous amount of tea into the pot. 'Then it's time for a change.'

'But *what*? I can't do anything else.'

'You're surely not so old that you can't learn something new,' said Mairi astringently. 'There was never anything wrong with your brains.'

'You mean, have a complete change?'

'You must have a wee bit of money in the bank. Though it's always worried me how generous you've been with us, I was afraid you weren't keeping enough for yourself. If you need money, I haven't spent the half of it. The rest is nicely in the bank, and I can take it out anytime you need it.'

Impulsively Moira got up and hugged her mother. 'You don't have to do that, Mum, I've got lots of money. I always wanted you to spend it on yourself.'

'Now what would I be needing? Come along now, and have your tea. Living in that New York place, you've probably forgotten what a decent cup of tea is.'

Mairi's idea of a decent cup of tea was a brew the colour of dark toffee. Malcolm complained she never made it strong enough; he liked his breakfast tea to have been made the evening before and to have spent the night simmering on the stove. Certainly Moira had never been presented with a cup of tea like Malcolm's in New York. Adding extra milk to her cup, she mused, 'I could go to university, I suppose. Start something entirely new. Although it's a shame to waste everything I've learned.'

'Archie MacNeil next door, he never married, you know,' said Mairi obliquely.

'No, Mum. I can't marry Archie,' Moira said firmly.

Mairi subsided. 'You could open a fancy shop. Sell the kind of clothes you usually wear.'

'That's what models often end up doing. That or a

share in a restaurant. But I'd have to do that in New York.' Her mouth drooped unconsciously.

'So what's suddenly wrong with New York? All these years you've talked about it as the nearest place to heaven.'

'*I* don't know, Mum . . . I'm so confused. I've been so unhappy at my job the last few months. And . . . and I've met a man,' she finished in a rush.

'About time. Is he a good man?'

She thought of Patrick's fierce devotion to his craft, his wit and sensitivity, his sudden fits of temper and his underlying integrity. 'Yes, he's a good man. He wants to marry me, Mum.'

As usual, Mairi dealt with the essentials. 'Do you love him?'

'Yes,' said Moira in blank astonishment. 'Yes, I do.' Her face broke into an ecstatic smile. 'I really do! Why did I have to come here to realise that?'

'I have no idea. What is his name?'

Her words falling all over themselves, her face lit with an inner glow, Moira poured out the story of Patrick's brief, turbulent courtship. When she described his house in New Brunswick, she was careful to mention the separate bedrooms; that she herself did not want that situation to continue she kept to herself. 'The trouble is, he only spends two months a year in New York and the rest in New Brunswick, and my schedule would be the exact reverse.'

'In my day a young woman was happy to stay home and mind the house . . . and the babies.'

Moira got up to get more tea, more to avoid Mairi's all-too-discerning gaze than from any desire for another cup of what tasted like straight tannic acid. 'If we had a baby, I would stay home,' she mumbled. 'At least until it started school. But I need a job of my own. Patrick's busy a lot of the time.' Which was something of a euphemism, she thought, remembering the litter of papers on his desk and the fight over the two uneaten meals.

'Is he the reason you seem so different? You know, Maura,' the old name slipped out without Mairi noticing the difference, 'we haven't had a talk like this for a long time.'

'Too long, Mum. I'm sorry—it's been my fault. I was so determined to achieve my goals in New York and so single-minded about it that I cut myself off from other people and other places. You and Da and my home. I don't want to do that any more. Patrick told me how important one's roots are, and how one cuts oneself off from them at one's peril.'

Mairi nodded. 'He said that, did he? He'll do,' she said, which from her was high praise. 'You must bring him here to meet us. You'll tell your da about him this evening?'

'Will he approve of me being in love with a man who writes plays for his living? Patrick's not Archie, Mum.'

'He'll make a lot of noise and he'll ask a lot of questions,' Mairi said philosophically. 'And he won't believe the man's good enough for you. In your da's eyes the man's not born yet who's good enough for you. Malcolm always thought the sun rose and set with you, Moira.'

'I've always been a bit scared of him,' Moira confessed. 'Remember how angry he was when I told him I was going to New York?'

'Your da likes to rant and rave, it's his way. And maybe if you worked underground all day in all that dust and noise, you'd want to bluster and shout a bit when you came up.'

'You still love him, don't you? After all these years.'

Mairi was not one to talk about love. She sniffed. 'He's been a good man to me.'

'Come on, Mum, say it. You love Da.'

Mairi got up and bustled over to the stove. 'Well, what if I do now? It's nothing to make a song and dance about.'

Moira chuckled. 'You're not nearly as hard as you sound. Oh, Mum, it's good to be home!'

Mairi turned and looked her daughter straight in the eye. 'It's good to have you home.' She wiped her hands briskly on her print apron, which covered an equally shapeless print house dress. 'I got some nice fresh fish from the wharf for supper.'

'Haddock fillets? Will you fry them?'

'I thought I might. And I made a lemon meringue pie for dessert.'

'All my favourites. I'll get fat.'

Mairi looked at her daughter's slim curves disparagingly. 'Wouldn't hurt you to put some weight on. A man likes a woman to have a bit of flesh on her bones.'

Patrick likes me as I am ... not a thought to share with Mairi, but rather one to be hugged to herself. 'What can I do to help?'

Moira ate too much supper, dried the dishes, unpacked her suitcase, and settled into her old room under the eaves. The faded pink roses on the wallpaper, the white-painted bed, the lumpy mattress were all the same. And then from downstairs came the creak of the back door and the thump of her father's footsteps in the porch. That, too, was the same. Feeling her nerves tighten, she ran downstairs.

Malcolm MacLeod was hanging up his jacket in the back porch. He was wearing green serge trousers and a matching shirt, for the miners left their working gear at the pithead when they showered. He was a heavyset, big-boned man, his grizzled hair cropped close to his head, his jowled face still showing a vestige of the handsome, black-browed young man who had won the heart of the grey-eyed Mairi.

In her socked feet Moira had made no sound crossing the kitchen floor. 'Hello, Da,' she said.

Hands on his hips, Malcolm looked her up and down. 'Have you quit your job?' he growled. 'How come you're not all dressed up?'

Patrick had pointed out how she had used her elegant Fifth Avenue wardrobe and her faultless grooming to keep a distance between her and her parents; to hide behind when she came back to the town where she had been born. Ashamed of herself, she now realised how well her ploy had worked, for her father was looking at her as if he could not believe his eyes. 'I haven't quit my job yet—but I may,' she said.

Slowly he nodded his head. 'You look like my Maura again. Come here, girl.' She padded across the floor towards him. He rested his big hands on her shoulders; his eyes, still black-rimmed with coal dust, were on a level with hers. Very quietly he added, 'And more like my Mairi then you ever have before.'

Moira's eyes flooded with tears. 'Oh, Da . . .'

He threw his arms around her, squeezed her so tightly she feared for the safety of her rib cage, and kissed her somewhere in the vicinity of her nose. Then he lifted her into the kitchen and dumped her back on her feet, his grin splitting his face. 'Mind you, you'll never be half the woman your mother was—eh, Mairi?'

Mairi was turning fish cakes in the cast iron frying pan on the stove. 'You take off your work boots, Malcolm MacLeod,' she scolded. 'Walking all over my clean kitchen floor, indeed.' But her cheeks were pink from more than the heat of the stove, and Malcolm winked at his daughter as he tiptoed back to the door and began unlacing his size twelve boots.

'Fish cakes smell good,' he said pacifically. 'Tea made?'

Moira said pertly, 'At least an hour ago by the look of it—it's black as tar. Drinking that stuff must be terribly bad for you, Da.'

'A good cup of tea never hurt anyone.' As Malcolm sat down at the table, Mairi gave him an ample helping of fish cakes, which he proceeded to cover with ketchup. Only when he was served did she sit down herself. Once this would have annoyed Moira. Now she was readier to understand that Malcolm's job was at the coal face, Mairi's in the kitchen; that Mairi did not get paid for her job in no way denigrated it in her own eyes or those of her husband.

Malcolm buttered a thick slab of homemade bread. 'You thinking of leaving New York?'

Faltering at first, for she had always found her father more formidable to talk to than her mother, Moira began to describe her gradual disillusion with the career she had fought so hard to establish. Then, as Malcolm tackled a piece of lemon pie and a second mug of tea, she said bravely, 'I've met a man called Patrick Casey. He wants me to marry him.'

Malcolm slammed his mug down on the tablecloth. 'Does he now?' he roared. 'And just who the hell is this Patrick Casey?'

'Malcolm!' said his wife in automatic reproof.

Normally Malcolm respected Mairi's proscription on swearing. Taking a deep breath Moira said, 'He's a well-known playwright. His plays——'

'Plays!' Malcolm interrupted with as much horror as if Moira had said Patrick was a brothel-keeper.

'Yes, plays, Da. Public performances in a theatre, that people pay money to see.'

'What's wrong with you marrying a decent coal miner? There's young Archie next door still eating his heart out over you. *Plays* . . .'

'Patrick knows how to split wood, Da. And run a tractor and make maple syrup,' Moira said mischievously.

'And does he ride the tractor down the streets of New York?'

'He lives in New Brunswick.'

Somewhat mollified, Malcolm took a gulp of tea. 'But he doesn't have a steady job. Apart from these plays.'

'His plays have been on Broadway for the last seven or eight years. He makes more money from his writing than—than the president of the coal company.'

Malcolm glowered at her from beneath his brows. 'Don't have me on now, girl—this is a serious matter, a young man after my daughter's hand. And where is he, anyway? He should be here knocking on my door, asking my permission, that's where he should be.'

'I haven't accepted yet,' she said meekly. 'If I do, you'll be the first person to meet him.'

'So why are you dilly-dallying? Does he not make enough money for you now that you're a famous model?'

'I'm trying to explain that,' she said patiently. 'He lives in New Brunswick most of the year and I live in New York. That's one reason I'm dilly-dallying.'

'If he's a decent man, then you quit your job and go where he is. *Is* he a decent man, Maura?'

She answered seriously, 'Yes, he is. You'll like him. He'll give you back as good as you give him, mind you.' She smiled reminiscently. 'We've had some rousing fights.'

'That's what you need, my girl. A man who'll stand up to you and not take any of your nonsense.'

'Archie never stood up to me, Da. I could trample all over Archie and he'd still come back for more.'

'Think you're smart, don't you?' Malcolm gave her a grudging smile. 'Archie is a bit that way inclined, I'll grant you. So when's the wedding?'

'I—I haven't accepted him yet. I told you that.'

'Good men don't grow on trees. And you're not getting any younger, you know. Alan was born and Ewan on the way when your mother was your age.'

'I'm not quite over the hill, Da!'

'There'll be none of this foolishness like living together.' Malcolm's eyebrows came into play again. 'You know how I feel about that. Your get a wedding ring on your finger, girl, that's my advice to you.'

She lowered her eyes. 'Yes, Da.'

Satisfied, Malcolm shoved back his chair and stretched. 'Guess I'll watch TV for a while. You help your mother with the dishes, Maura.'

'Yes, Da,' she repeated, struggling against a smile as Malcolm left the room. The meeting between Malcolm and Patrick—if it took place, of course, she added hastily—should be well worth watching. She rolled up her sleeves and carried her father's plates over to the sink.

CHAPTER THIRTEEN

THREE days later Archie came to call. Moira was upstairs helping her mother with some spring-cleaning; she had a scarf wrapped around her hair and was wearing an old pair of jeans that had belonged to Ewan in his younger days but which were none the less too big for Moira. Her T-shirt, which had also belonged to Ewan, suggested in large black letters that the wearer should be hugged. Mairi had not approved of a son of hers wearing such a T-shirt.

Pulling open the back door, Moira looked all the way up into Archie's eyes, which were several inches above her own. Archie must be taller than Patrick, she decided; but Archie had none of Patrick's looseknit grace. Archie treated his hands and feet as distantly placed appendages for whose movements he was not wholly responsible. She said, smiling at him with sincere warmth, 'Hello, Archie. How nice to see you.'

He had light blond hair slicked to one side, and very fair skin which had a tendency to blush. It did so now. 'Hello, Moira.'

She had always felt he called her Moira in an effort to please, not because he liked the name. 'Come in.'

He twisted his cap in his hands. 'Today's my day off. Would you like to go to the movies tonight?'

She put her head to one side. 'Love to. What time?'

'Eight o'clock? I'll call for you.'

'Okay.' She grinned at him, wishing he would relax. 'I'll make sure I change!'

He looked down at her outfit, read the injunction on the T-shirt, and blushed again. 'You look fine to me,' he mumbled.

You must be blind, she thought ironically. 'Is it okay if I wear jeans! I only brought casual clothes.'

154

'Sure.'

He would have said sure if she'd suggested wearing an evening dress and diamonds. 'I'll see you later. Thanks, Archie.'

As she closed the door on his retreating back, she wondered if she was doing the right thing. She certainly should not be encouraging Archie, there was no point in that.

The movie, which was called *Romancing the Stone*, was a light-hearted spoof in which the heroine, a writer of romantic fiction, was plunged into the jungles of Colombia along with the hero, a treasure map, an egg-sized emerald, a kidnapped sister, an assortment of villains from the comical to the sinister, and altogether too many ravenous alligators. Moira was heartily entertained; she was still chuckling over some of the heroine's exploits as she and Archie ordered coffee and dessert in a nearby restaurant. While they were waiting for their order, she began questioning Archie about his family and his work, gradually drawing him out to talk about himself and his aspirations. She was a good listener; Archie became, for him, loquacious. Finally she interjected with just the right touch of lightness, 'You haven't mentioned a girlfriend in all this, Archie.'

'That's because there isn't one.'

'No?' With seeming irrelevance she added, 'Whatever happened to Lorraine MacAllister? Is she still around?' All through high school Lorraine had been as much in love with Archie as Archie had been with Moira.

'She trained as a nurse and works at the hospital.'

'She'd be an excellent nurse. Caring but firm. She never married?' Archie shook his head. Moira made quite a business of adding cream and sugar to her coffee as she went on, with apparent nonchalance, 'I suppose I'm being egotistical. I happen to have met the man I'd like to marry, so I think everyone else should be in the same boat. May I tell you about him?' *I'm doing this to be kind, Archie. Believe me.*

'Yes,' said Archie stiffly.

'His name is Patrick Casey. He's a playwright who lives in New Brunswick most of the time, New York occasionally. Next time I come home I'll probably bring him with me.' *And isn't it better that you're forwarned?*

She risked a glance at her companion. He was staring at his Black Forest cake as if he wasn't sure what it was, let alone how it got there. Swiftly she covered his hand with hers. 'Archie, I could never belong in Scots Bay again.'

'Never belong with me, you mean.'

'Both, I guess.' This was not turning out quite as she had hoped. 'I've really enjoyed my visit this time. I'm closer to Mum and Da than I have been for years, and I've finally allowed myself to recognise how much I owe to this town. My roots are here and always will be. But that doesn't mean that I want to live here.'

'I always hoped you'd get New York out of your system and come back home.'

To me, he meant. 'That won't happen, Archie. I was so anxious to get away from Scots Bay that I used to see only the good in New York and none of the bad—I couldn't admit to anyone that life in the big city was anything less than perfect. I'm not like that anymore. The perfect place probably hasn't been invented. Or else I haven't discovered it yet. But that still doesn't mean that I'll come back to Scots Bay.'

'So you're going to marry this guy and live in New Brunswick?'

'I don't know where we're going to live—that's one of the problems. But I can't imagine marrying anyone else.'

'Will he be good to you?'

Essentially it was the same question her father had asked. 'Yes,' she said simply.

His face was pinched and pale. 'I hope you'll be happy.'

Her hand was still covering his. 'Archie, I'm sorry. I've hurt you, haven't I, and I didn't want to do that. But I thought it would hurt you worse if I suddenly arrived on your doorstep with a husband in tow.'

'It would have—you're right.' He managed a smile. 'I'll get over it.'

She put all the force she could in her words. 'You must, Archie. Because I'm not available.'

'I get the message,' he said stolidly.

'In the next couple of weeks, give Lorraine a call. I bet she'd be happy to hear from you. And now, before you tell me I'm an interfering bitch, I'm going to be quiet and mind my own business.'

Archie looked shocked. 'I'd never tell you that.'

Thank heavens Patrick didn't idolise her! Patrick would call her whatever he thought she deserved; Patrick knew she had a temper and was perfectly prepared to deal with it. 'Well, I can be interfering and a bitch, I assure you.' She smiled at him. 'Shall we go? Mum and I are tackling the spare bedroom tomorrow, so I don't want to be too late home. If I have half the energy she has when I'm her age, I'll be doing all right.'

They drove home. Archie stopped outside her house and walked her to the door. Knowing he would not take the initiative, Moira reached up and kissed him on the cheek. 'Goodbye, Archie. Be happy.' Turning quickly, she let herself in. She had been right to tell Archie about Patrick, for Archie had been in love with a dream-woman for far too long; but she still felt as if she'd ground a small, helpless creature into the earth with her heel. A ridiculous simile for a man the size of Archie, but there it was.

'That you, Maura?'

'Yes, Da.' Just so had her father shouted at her as a teenager when she had been out on a date.

'That man of yours phoned. Wants you to call him back.'

She hurried into the kitchen. 'Is everything all right?'

Malcolm peered at her over his glasses. 'I guess so. Though he didn't sound best pleased when I told him you were out with Archie.'

'Da! I suppose you told him Archie's been in love with me for years—really!'

'Don't want him taking you for granted.'

The only telephone in the house was in the kitchen. 'Wouldn't you like to take your paper into the living room?' she asked pointedly.

'Too cold. I'll turn my back.'

Her fingers moving with angry jerks, she dialled Patrick's number. He answered on the first ring. 'Hello.'

Not an encouraging tone of voice. 'It's Moira.'

'So you're home. Who were you out with?'

'The boy next door.'

'The one your parents want you to marry?'

'That's right.'

'Didn't take you long to arrange that.'

'*He* asked *me*, Patrick. You're jealous.'

'Damn right I am. Was that your father I spoke to?'

'Yes. He's sitting ten feet away from me listening to every word.'

'He seemed very ready to tell me you were out with someone else.'

'He doesn't think you should take me for granted.'

'Darling Moira, I'm not about to do that. So what did you do all evening?'

'We went to a movie and then we talked about you.'

She heard the humming of the connection, then Patrick said drily, 'As a cue, that's far too obvious, Moira. However, I shall oblige. What did you say?'

Too late she saw where she was headed. 'You've got to understand that Archie has been in love with me—or at least with an idealised picture of me—for years. I told him I'd met you, and that he was wasting his time. I didn't put it quite that bluntly, but that was the gist of it.'

'Did you tell him you were going to marry me?'

'I told him I might,' she blurted.

'Oh, did you—so he's more up to date than I am.'

She knew that dangerously silky note in his voice. 'I also told him to phone up the girl who's been in love with him since high school days and ask her for a date.'

Patrick's voice sounded better already. 'What an interfering creature you are.'

'I thought so, too. He didn't. He thinks everything I do is marvellous.'

'Very bad for you, that attitude. You'll never catch me thinking that.'

'You mean you don't think I'm perfect?' she asked in mock dismay.

'Some things about you are perfect. Would you like this to turn into an obscene phone call while I describe them to you?'

'No!' she said in a strangled voice. 'Not right now.'

'Your father wouldn't appreciate that, eh? Too bad . . . which brings me to the reason I called, Moira. Kit's come to stay for a week. She and the boys will be here when you get back. So we'll have to behave ourselves.'

'Oh,' she said blankly.

'Sorry, darling. Her timing's atrocious. But I didn't have the heart to turn her down.'

'How is she?'

'Actually, much better than she was two weeks ago. I think she cried so much then that she got a lot of it out of her system.'

'Are you disappointed?' Moira asked in a neutral tone of voice, and she was not referring to Kit's emotional health.

'I dream about you every night and wake up aching to hold you. Yes, I'm disappointed.'

'Me, too,' she said helplessly.

'Well . . . how are you keeping busy all day?'

'House-cleaning and eating too much.' They chatted a few minutes longer, then Patrick said, 'I've got your flight time. I'll be at the airport to meet you.'

'That will be lovely.' She forgot about her father, forgot everything but the utter certainty of the emotion that filled her. 'Patrick, I love you,' she said.

Behind her the newspaper rattled loudly. When Patrick spoke, she knew immediately how deeply moved he was. 'I love you, too.'

Moira could think of nothing to say. She hung on to the receiver while the miles hummed between them, wishing with all her heart that she could see his face and feel the warmth of his hands. In the end Patrick broke the silence. 'It's the first time you've said those words to me. You realise you've made me feel about ten feet tall?'

She gave a delighted laugh. 'Have I?'

'At least. I could take on the whole world single-handed right now.'

'Don't chop any wood—that's all I ask!'

'I still look like the aftermath of a bar-room brawl. My love, I could talk to you all night, but I have the feeling your father may be getting impatient.'

'He is.'

'Sleep well and I'll see you soon.'

As she replaced the receiver, Malcolm cleared his throat. Moira forestalled him, saying brightly, 'I'll write you a cheque to cover the cost of the call, Da. And now I'd better go to bed—Mum wants to tear apart the spare bedroom tomorrow. Night.' She dropped a kiss on his grizzled head and ran for the stairs.

Moira hardly slept at all her last night in Scots Bay, because she was worrying about all the contingencies, meteorological and otherwise, that could prevent her from seeing Patrick the next day. Fog, wind, snow, ice. Mechanical failure, fuel shortage, pilots' strike. The list was unending; her need to see him a frightening, almost obsessive, unease. She would not feel whole until his arms were around her.

Her anxiety was for nothing. The plane touched down on the Moncton runway three minutes ahead of schedule. Moira laced her boots, pulled on her gloves, and needlessly checked her make-up. The plane taxied up to the gate. Her seat was midway along the cabin. In a fever of impatience she watched as all the passengers ahead of her struggled for their coats, hauled their baggage from under the seats and jockeyed for position in the aisle. The baby that had been screaming for the past thirty minutes continued to scream. The man sitting next to her was a car salesman, whose Dale Carnegie-style advances she had politely repulsed; he retaliated now by letting her get her own jacket out of the overhead compartment, his eyes on the lift of her breasts under her sweater. She contrived to step on his foot, saying falsely, 'Oh, I'm *so* sorry.'

She inched along the aisle towards the door, where the stewardesses were doling out professional smiles. 'Thank you. *Merci*. Goodbye. *Au revoir*.' The car salesman made a jocular remark; the blonde stewardess laughed, albeit hollowly. Not wanting to be anywhere near the man, Moira lagged behind a little. Finally, jostled by the other passengers, she was herded into the waiting area.

She saw Patrick immediately, for he was taller than average and not a man whose looks could easily be ignored. He was standing at the fringe of the crowd, his head of black hair inches above the rest of the people, his piercing blue eyes scanning the passengers for her arrival. Then he saw her. His eyes lit up. His tall, lean body began shouldering through the throng to reach her.

Moira stood still, her heart thumping as if she had been running, her eyes shining like lakewater shot with sunlight. Patrick edged around an overweight couple who were blocking his path, avoided two little boys who were playing tag around a pile of suitcases, and squeezed past an Acadian family that ranged from white-haired grandmothers to babes in arms.

He covered the last few feet in two long strides. Taking Moira by the shoulders, his gaze devouring her face, he demanded, 'I wasn't dreaming, was I? You did tell me on the telephone that you loved me?'

Trust Patrick to go straight to the heart of the matter. 'You weren't dreaming.'

'I've been totally useless all day—couldn't concentrate on anything until I saw you again. Moira, I love you so much it frightens me.'

'I love you, too,' she whispered. Then they were

locked in each other's arms and Patrick's mouth had found hers, and everything, crowds, suitcases, and Acadian grandmothers vanished from Moira's consciousness. There was only Patrick, the strength of his arms, the hunger of his kiss, the remembered contours of his body.

From behind them a voice piped, 'Uncle Pat, Uncle Pat, the baggage thing's started to go round.'

Unhurriedly Patrick released Moira. She looked down to see hazel eyes topped by a tangle of blond curls, and a small face screwed up with excitement and impatience. Patrick said, 'Cool it, Pete. Where's your mother?' So this was Peter, intrepid explorer of culverts.

A red-haired woman was standing diffidently to one side, a woman whose thin, attractive features and blue eyes were somehow familiar to Moira. The photograph on the bookshelves in Patrick's apartment . . . this must be his sister Kit. Kit was looking a little pinched about the mouth, and with compunction Moira realised that what had been a joyful reunion for herself and Patrick had probably been a poignant reminder of happier days for Kit.

Detaching herself from Patrick's embrace, Moira walked over to the red-haired woman, holding out her hand, her beauty a glowing, vibrant statement in the bare, utilitarian room. 'Hello, Kit,' she said. 'I'm so happy to meet you.'

Kit shook hands, her smile banishing the unhappiness from her mouth. 'Pat told me you'd be the most beautiful woman I'd ever seen—he wasn't exaggerating.'

Before Moira could reply, Peter grabbed at Kit's jacket. 'Mum, the suitcases are arriving. Can't we go and watch?'

'Peter, this is Miss Tennant. Moira, my son Peter.'

'Hello, Peter. Please call me Moira, okay?'

Peter solemnly shook her hand. 'Are you the lady Uncle Pat's going to marry?'

'I—I don't know. Maybe.'

'I've never been to a wedding. Will you invite me?'

Kit's exasperated, 'Peter . . .' was overriden by Moira's amused, 'If there is one, you shall certainly be invited.'

'Uncle Pat said you were going to marry him.'

Over Peter's head Moira glared at Patrick. 'Uncle Pat should keep his mouth shut.'

'Daniel's too young to go. He's only one.'

Daniel, Moira recalled, was the younger of Kit's two sons. She said drily, 'He might be older by the time we get married.

'Not by much,' Patrick interposed, an edge of steel in his voice.

Moira raised her chin. But before she could make a suitably scathing reply, Peter demanded, 'What colour's your suitcase?'

'Dark brown. I'd better come and show you.'

A few minutes later the four of them were walking out of the terminal into a day of crisp blue sky and bright sun, whose rays were not yet strong enough to defeat the chill of the wind. As they crossed the road, Moira saw the red Toyota in the parking lot. 'Did you leave Daniel in the car?' she said doubtfully.

'No, Dave's looking after him,' Patrick answered. 'We'll have to go straight home, because Dave has to go out at three. I'll drive, shall I, Kit?'

'Sure. Peter and I will sit in the back. I hope you didn't mind being met by such a deputation, Moira, but Peter loves airports and was dying to meet you.'

'Of course not—I'm flattered!' In one way it was true, and certainly Moira would not have hurt Kit's feelings for the world; in another way, she longed to be alone with Patrick, to be kissed and held until the blood raced in her veins and her body trembled with desire. That, she knew, would have to wait. In Scots Bay it had seemed a simple matter to wait a few days longer; in Moncton, with Patrick in the seat beside her, it was not nearly so simple.

Patrick was backing out of the parking space. She said tentatively, 'Your face looks better.'

Lightly he touched the narrow red line on his cheek. 'I dropped into the hospital on the way here, and they took the stitches out. Figured it saved a trip. Peter had to be forcibly restrained from accompanying me—bloodthirsty little wretch.'

'I only wanted to know how the doctor did it. Did he use scissors, Uncle Pat?'

'I have no idea, my eyes were shut,' Patrick said firmly. 'Tell me about your visit, Moira.'

She obliged, and the journey went quickly. Dave relinquished Daniel with some reluctance, which as the child was deposited on Moira's knee she could understand. Daniel was chubby with a red cowlick and large unwinking grey eyes that observed the world with the sobriety of a judge. He stared at Moira for a full two minutes, then gave her a gap-toothed, charming smile. Twin dimples popped out in his cheeks. Said Moira solemnly, 'You're perfectly gorgeous. You know it too, don't you? The girls are going to love you in a few years' time.'

Daniel waved his fat fists in the air, unloosed a string of gibberish, then waited for her reply, his eyes glued expectantly to her face. She said, 'If I were twenty years younger I'd give those girls a run for their money.'

'Ageing Playwright Abandoned for Younger Nephew,' Patrick intoned.

She rested her cheek on his shoulder. 'Not a hope.'

The house on the hill seemed very full of people that evening. Kit had prepared dinner ahead of time. They ate in the dining room, then Moira played cards with Peter, Daniel was bathed and put to bed, then later, reluctantly, Peter followed suit. The three adults sat around the fire in the living room chatting lazily; at ten o'clock Moira abandoned the attempt to stop yawning and said sleepily, 'I've had it—got to go to bed. Good night, Kit. Night, Patrick.' He was sitting with his feet up; she bent and kissed him, and hurried to her room. Apart from the kiss at the airport, he had been very circumspect in his behaviour towards her. She understood his reasons; yet, as she closed her bedroom door and started to undress, she also remembered that tonight should have been the night they made love. The bed looked big and empty. She fled into the bathroom to brush her teeth.

When she came back, Patrick had walked into her room and was closing the door behind him. He was fully dressed. She was wearing the nightgown she had described to him on the telephone in Phoenix, the one with the minimal bodice and the see-through skirt; she hitched ineffectually at the bodice and said irritably, 'Really, Patrick—what will Kit think?'

'She's gone to bed.'

'Then so should you—but not here.'

'I did not come here to go to bed with you.' He looked her up and down. 'Delightful though that might be. I came to ask you a question. When are you going to marry me, Moira?'

She crossed her arms over her breast. '*I* don't know.'

He took a step closer. 'That's not good enough.'

'It happens to be the truth. I *don't* know.'

'Then perhaps I should rephrase the question,' he said levelly. 'Do you want to marry me, Moira?'

Her answer came instinctively, without thought. 'Yes.'

He let out his breath in a long sigh. 'Well, that's something, I suppose. So why don't we settle on a date?'

In a spurt of anger she said, 'You're showing about as much emotion as if you were setting up an appointment with your agent.'

'If I deal with this any other way, you know and I know where we'll end up.'

She kept her eyes averted from the bed. 'How can we settle on a date when we don't even know where we're going to live?'

'I think we should get married first and worry about that afterwards.'

'We can't, Patrick!'

He had thrust his hands in the pockets of his jeans; his shoulders were hunched. 'Why the hell not?'

'Because I will not undertake a marriage in which we have to live hundreds of miles apart.'

'You're so bloody rational.'

'One of us has to be.' She did not feel rational; she felt angry and upset and horribly frustrated.

'Head over heart? Brain over body? Let's see how deep it goes, darling Moira.'

'Patrick, stay away——'

He did not use his superior strength, nor was he rough or brutal. He simply covered her mouth with his own, letting his hands gently clasp her hips.

With brain and will Moira fought against her body's weakness; when Patrick let her go, his hands lingering at the curve of her waist, she was scarlet-cheeked and trembling. But her arms were still crossed over her breast.

'You're going to marry me,' Patrick said softly. 'Come hell or high water.'

Shakily she replied, 'Cliché, Patrick.'

'All I'm capable of at the moment. Cliché or no, I mean every word of it.'

With the last shred of her resolve she said, 'I won't marry you and live apart two-thirds of the year.'

He looked as if he would rather throttle her than make love to her. 'By God, you're stubborn!'

'Then I'm a good match for you.'

'You're getting your priorities wrong, Moira.' His voice had that dangerous silkiness she had encountered once or twice before. 'What's between you and me is rarer than you may think. Whatever fates there are were kind enough to bring us together—we'll regret it for the rest of our lives if we throw away our chance to love each other, just because we can't sort out a minor detail like where we're going to live. You might do well to remember that.'

He gave her a cool nod, neither touching her nor attempting to kiss her good night. She watched him open the door and step into the hall. The latch clicked shut behind him. Her shoulders were aching with tension; slowly she lowered her arms to her sides.

Moira discovered the next morning that Kit was not blind to the undercurrents between herself and Patrick. Kit and Daniel were in the kitchen when Moira trailed in at nine o'clock. 'I'm not usually this late,' Moira confessed. 'I think my mother wore me out. We house-cleaned the place from top to bottom while I was there.'

'I hadn't expected you to go to bed so early last night—I'd fully intended leaving you and Patrick alone for a while. I shouldn't even be here, you don't need a third person around.'

Kit was busily stirring the scrambled eggs. Moira said urgently, 'Please don't feel that way, Kit. Patrick has told me about you, and I'm so happy that you're here.' With sudden insight she added, 'I'm sure the evenings are difficult for you.'

'They are. I'm okay during the day when the boys are around. But once they're in bed, I—I miss Sandy. No adult conversation. No one sitting across from you . . .' Her voice was low. 'No one to go to bed with.'

Kit had Patrick's tendency to plunge into intimacy. 'You must stay as long as you want to,' Moira said gently. 'Patrick and I have lots of time.' Although Patrick might not agree with her statement.

'That's what *I* thought. I thought Sandy and I had all our lives ahead of us. But we didn't. Don't waste time, you and Patrick. Because you never know what might happen tomorrow.' Kit's thin face was passionate with pleading.

Moira put two slices of bread in the toaster, deciding to match intimacy with intimacy. 'Would you ever marry again?'

'If you'd asked me a couple of weeks ago, I'd have said no. But I got a lot of the grief and anger off my chest those few days that Patrick stayed with me, and now I'm almost sure I would. Eventually. If I found the right man.'

'Are you dating at all?'

'Not yet. It doesn't seem to feel right.' Kit spooned eggs into Daniel's bowl. 'But I can see that I might in a while.' She pulled a face. 'Not that anyone would look at me right now. I've really let myself go, it all seemed too much effort.'

In a single expert glance Moira took in Kit's pale, early-morning face, untidy brows and split ends. 'Tell you what—why don't you let me trim and set your hair this morning, and make up your face.'

'Would you?' Kit looked like a little girl promised a treat. 'That would be such fun—you're a real pro! Not that I'll ever look anywhere near as beautiful as you.'

Moira busied herself buttering the toast. 'By the time I've finished with you this morning, I'll have a rival.'

'You'll have to be a magician!' More seriously, Kit added, 'I'm so glad to have met you, Moira, and I'm very happy for you and Patrick—it's okay, Daniel, it's still too hot. I've never seen Patrick like this before. He was always sort of cool and in control as far as women were concerned, never in any danger of losing his head. Or his heart. He's certainly not like that with you.'

Cool and in control were not words Moira would have used to describe Patrick. 'Does it last, Kit? Love, I mean.'

'It changes.' Kit began ladling eggs into Daniel's open mouth. 'That first euphoric, head-over-heels-in-love stage settles into a deeper, more trusting kind of relationship. Or it did with me and Sandy.' She smiled reminiscently. 'We had our fights, mind you. I don't have red hair for nothing, and he could be *so* stubborn. But we had an unwritten rule that we never let the sun go down on our anger. And making up could be a lot of fun!'

'Patrick and I seem to fight a lot, too.'

'I'm glad you're not a doormat,' said his sister severely. 'That would be very bad for him.'

Said Patrick from the doorway, 'No danger of that.'

Kit and Moira both jumped, Daniel's eggs missed his

mouth and rolled down his bib, and he wailed a protest. 'Really, Pat,' Kit said crossly, 'you're not supposed to listen to other people's conversations.'

'How can I help it when they're about me?' Patrick said with indisputable logic. 'Enough coffee for me to have some?' He walked over to Moira, who was rooted to the spot, and deposited a kiss on her nose. 'Morning, darling.'

Her heart, always unpredictable in his vicinity, turned over with love for him, and the last vestige of her anger vanished. 'Good morning. Have you had breakfast?'

'I certainly have. I was in the study by seven-thirty,' he said smugly. He poured himself a coffee and added cream and sugar. 'Where's Peter, Kit?'

'He's playing outside.'

Patrick glanced out of the window over the sink. 'Oh, there he is, by the woodpile.' His voice sharpened. 'What the devil is he doing?'

'Probably looking for Indian relics, it's his latest craze,' Kit said placidly, shovelling more egg into Daniel's ever-open mouth.

But Patrick wasn't listening. He swung round from the sink and made a dash for the door. It slammed shut behind him. Suddenly afraid, Moira hurried to the window and looked out. For a moment she saw nothing to cause alarm: hunkered down by the woodpile, Peter was tugging away at something at its base. But then she saw what Patrick had seen. Peter had pulled enough chunks of wood from the bottom of the heap that the logs over his head were in danger of falling on him.

Her fingers gripped the edge of the counter so hard that the tendons stood out on the back of her hand. As if a silent movie were being played in front of her eyes, she watched Patrick race across the dead brown grass towards the woodpile, grab Peter and fling him to one side just as the maple and birch logs came crashing downwards. Then Patrick's foot slipped on a patch of ice. He was thrown off balance with his leg twisted at an awkward angle. His body thudded to the ground.

With an inarticulate whimper of fear, Moira brushed past Kit and fumbled for the door handle. Her body would not obey her; all her actions seemed to be in slow motion. She stumbled across the grass, and only later would realise she had irretrievably ruined a pair of slippers. Patrick was lying face down, absolutely still. Dead still, she thought in sick wordless terror. And in that instant she discovered something. Patrick had been right: what was between them was rare and precious, and infinitely to be valued. Nothing else mattered but their love for each other ... not careers or money or houses.

She dropped to her knees. 'Patrick! Oh God, Patrick, are you all right?'

He groaned, and it was the most wonderful sound she had ever heard in her life. Then he tried to move his legs, and uttered a single pithy word that hopefully did not reach his nephew's ears. Raising himself on his elbows, he gave his head a shake. 'Done something to my ankle,' he mumbled. 'Is Peter okay?'

Peter, Moira now realised, was standing beside them, his face paper-white, his eyes huge. 'All the logs fell down,' he said with awe. 'Did they hurt you, Uncle Pat?'

'My only injury was self-inflicted when I slipped on the ice,' Patrick grunted. 'Not one of my more heroic exploits.' With commendable restraint he added, 'What were you looking for, Pete?'

'Arrows and bones.'

'Arrowheads and bones are buried underground, not in newly split wood. You might keep that in mind in future.'

'Yes, Uncle Pat.' The child's lip trembled. 'I didn't mean to hurt you.'

By now Kit had joined them, her face as pale as her son's. 'What happened?'

Patiently Patrick explained, finishing, 'I'm sure he won't do it again—so don't read the riot act, Sis. Can the two of you help me up?'

Although she was dizzy with relief and an in-
expressible gratitude, Moira managed to say com-
posedly, 'We'll have to get you in the Toyota. You do
realise this means another trip to the hospital?'

'Very bad technique to repeat oneself like that,'
Patrick muttered. 'Ready, you two?'

He could not bear any weight on the injured foot; the
small, animal-like sound of pain that was wrenched
from his lips as he stood upright told Moira that. They
were perhaps forty feet from the land cruiser. She said
in a thin voice, 'You hold him up, Kit. I'm going to
back the Toyota over here.'

Even so, getting Patrick into the front seat was a
nightmare from which he emerged with a grey face and
sweat-beaded forehead, and Moira with a sick
trembling throughout her entire body. Kit did not look
much better. She fetched Moira's handbag and shoes
from the house and waved goodbye as Moira
negotiated the ruts in the driveway.

Dr Reynolds was as breezy and full of bonhomie as
before; the ankle was declared to be sprained, not
broken; and Patrick was despatched homewards
bandaged and supplied with pain-killers and crutches.
He hobbled across the hospital parking lot to the
Toyota.

Moira opened the door on the passenger side,
glancing up at him as she did so. He was struggling with
one of the crutches, frowning in concentration; a lock
of raven hair had fallen over his forehead. Love twisted
her heart in its hands. She remembered that agonising
moment by the woodpile when she had thought he was
dead, and suddenly turned away, her vision blinded by
tears.

'Moira—what's wrong?'

'Nothing,' she choked.

'Darling, please look at me. I'll drop these bloody
crutches if I try to turn you round myself.'

She whirled, buried her contorted face in his chest
and wrapped her arms around him. 'When you fell, for

a minute I thought you were dead,' she sobbed. 'Patrick, I love you so much.'

He put his arms around her, rocking her gently back and forth until her weeping subsided. Then he said, his voice not quite steady, 'I love you, too. More than I can say.'

She scrubbed at her eyes. 'Will you fall flat on your face if I kiss you?'

'Probably—try me.'

Their kiss said all that words could not. Patrick did not fall over, although one of his crutches did. Moira bent to pick it up, helped him into the passenger seat, and they drove home.

The next day Patrick's ankle was considerably less swollen and not nearly as painful. He spent a couple of hours in the study in the morning, afterwards limping out on to the verandah where Moira and Kit were sitting in the sun with the two boys. 'I'm feeling cooped up,' he said. 'Why don't we get a sitter tonight and go to the movies?'

Kit said quickly, 'I'll stay with the boys. You two go.'

Simultaneously and with equal firmness Moira and Patrick said, 'No!'

'Okay, okay,' Kit said meekly. 'Maybe you could do my face today, Moira.'

'What's wrong with it?' Patrick asked.

'Moira's going to make a new woman out of me. Hair, make-up, the lot. I'll be like those before and after photos you see in magazines.'

'We'll definitely go out, then.'

Within five minutes Patrick had the sitter organised and was back in the study. After lunch, while Daniel was having his nap and Peter was sprawled on the floor with a book, Moira set to work. She knew her ability as a hairdresser was limited, so she contented herself with trimming Kit's hair to get rid of the split ends, and loosely turning the ends under with a curling iron. She had treated it with a conditioner; it looked smoother, shinier, sleeker, when she was finished. 'You should use conditioner every time you wash your hair.'

'Daniel always seems to wake up as soon as I put the shampoo on. So I end up rushing.'

Moira took her time with the make-up, the overall effect being soft and subtle rather than showy. A skilful use of blusher widened Kit's face and gave it a youthful glow, while eyeliner, mascara, and shadow transformed her from a harried-looking mother to a mysterious seductress. 'Your mouth is perfect,' Moira remarked, applying lip gloss with a tiny brush. 'There. That's got it. What do you think?'

Moira had purposely hidden the mirror until she had finished. She had her reward as Kit's eyes widened and her lips curved in a delightful—and astonished—smile. 'Wow! I've never looked like that before. Will you teach me how to do it myself?'

'Of course. It just takes practice.'

'I must go and show Patrick.' Carrying the mirror, entranced with her own reflection, Kit hurried across the hall, tapped on the study door, and walked in. Moira followed. Patrick was seated at his desk in front of the typewriter, and any impatience he might have felt at the interruption was dispelled by the sight of his sister's glowing, radiant face. He got up and limped over to her. 'You look lovely, Sis.'

Kit pirouetted so her hair flew out in a shining parabola. 'I do look nice, don't I?' she said naively.

'We'll have to hit the bars after the movie—can't waste that face.'

'Moira's going to show me how to do the make-up myself.'

Over Kit's head Patrick's blue eyes sent a silent message of thanks to the woman standing by the door. He knew it was more than a question of face powder and eyeshadow; he could see the pride and confidence in Kit's bearing, a confidence that had been sadly lacking for the last few months. And he was grateful.

CHAPTER FOURTEEN

THE movie was a re-run of an old Pink Panther film. Kit, Moira, and Patrick laughed all the way through it, and repaired to the bar in the Hotel Beausejour. A pianist was playing old-time favourites; a fire crackled in the hearth. Kit was abstracted, gazing around the dimly lit room at the other patrons. When Patrick chided her for inattention, she said, 'I've been thinking—and no funny remarks, brother dear. Moira, could you make up all the other women in this room?'

'The way I did you?' Kit nodded. Moira looked around her. 'Yes—it wouldn't be that difficult. It's a question of looking at a face to see the bad points and the good points, then making the least of the former and the most of the latter. Simple, really.'

Said Kit, even more thoughtfully, 'It didn't take you very long.'

'When I first started as a model, I used to do all my own make-up—I've never lost the knack. It's nothing to get excited about, Kit.'

'I think it is. Because I've just had an idea. You know what I think you should do? You should start up a chain of shops where you do make-up, hairstyling and manicures.'

'Elizabeth Arden already has,' Moira said, amused rather than interested.

'Not around here. And not for ordinary people. I don't mean for the rich, I mean for people like me. Single mothers who need a lift. Housewives who don't have much money but who would love to have their husbands give them a second and a third look.'

'A poor woman's Elizabeth Arden,' Moira joked.

'You're not taking me seriously, Moira! I *am* serious. I think you'd tap a whole new market.'

'There are already far too many beauty parlours.'

'Not beauty parlours run by a famous model. And anyway, most of their business is hairstyling. You'd be involved in more than that. You could even have exercise classes. Trim your waistline. Get rid of that bulge. Firm up your breasts. You know the sort of thing.'

'The total woman,' Moira said thoughtfully, beginning to pay more attention. 'Hair, face, nails, and body.'

'You could sell your own line of cosmetics, maybe eventually clothes. Start off with sportswear for the fitness classes and expand from there. Teach poise and grooming. There's no end to the possibilities.'

Moira was really listening now. 'I like the idea of it being for ordinary people. I'd have to keep my overheads down so I wouldn't price myself out of the market.'

'Your name associated with it would be a tremendous drawing card. I mean, look what you did for me today, Moira. I felt like a new woman when I looked in that mirror—it made a world of difference.'

Said Moira, excitely, 'That's what I could call it—"A World of Difference".'

'Wonderful!' Kit exclaimed. 'You'd have to have a location in Halifax. Then there's Moncton, St John, Fredericton, Charlottetown. Maybe Sydney. Some shops could be smaller than others. You'd have to visit them all on a rotating basis.'

'Where would I start?'

'Halifax, I would think. Wouldn't you, Patrick?'

He too had been listening attentively. 'It seems the logical place. You've got capital to invest, haven't you, Moira? And you were looking for a change of career. You'd have to do some market research first, of course, check the whole thing out. But I think Kit's right—your name would be a real drawing card. And you certainly have the practical know-how. Would the business end be a problem?'

'I could take some courses, do a lot of reading and research,' Moira said enthusiastically. 'You're probably not aware of how horribly bored I've been getting with my job, Kit—the idea of learning something new really appeals to me. A new challenge.'

Patrick laughed. 'Watch out, Kit—you're talking to the woman who went to New York at eighteen as an unknown, and became one of the top models in the country. Moira, if you wanted to start out in Halifax, we could rent a place along the south shore, by the ocean, until we saw if it was going to work out.'

'You mean you'd leave your house in Pleasantvale?' Moira said blankly.

'For a place by the ocean, yes.'

'But could you work there?'

'I'm sure I could. I wouldn't want to live in the city itself.'

'I could commute if we weren't too far from Halifax. And I could sell my house in New York. That would give me more money to invest.'

Said Patrick, 'We could get married.'

Moira beamed at him. 'I wouldn't have to live in New York any more.'

'We could live in the same house.'

'By the sea. And I could run my own business.'

Patrick stood up, leaning on the table for support. 'Will you marry me, Moira?'

She too stood up, her voice and smile exultant. 'We could live together, all year round! Oh, yes, I'd love to marry you, Patrick.'

The table between them, Patrick kissed her soundly. There was a smatter of applause from the nearby tables, a wolf whistle from the corner, and the pianist, sensing romance, struck up the wedding march. Dazedly Moira looked around her. 'An audience again. This must be the most public proposal on record.'

'At least I'll never be able to get out of it—too many witnesses.'

'I hope you'll never want to.'

He kissed her again. 'Believe me, I never will.' He signalled to the waitress, ordered champagne, and sat down. 'Congratulate us, Kit. She's finally agreed to marry me.'

'Finally—I've only known you for two-and-a-half months,' Moira protested. 'Oh Kit, how clever you were to come up with that idea! You've solved all our problems. I couldn't see how Patrick and I were ever going to be able to marry, because what in the world would I do with myself in Pleasantvale? But if I start my own business, we could manage just fine. Once it's established, I could probably run it from the house in Pleasantvale.' She frowned, already planning ahead. 'I'll have to train my staff very carefully . . .'

The cork popped from the champagne bottle and solemnly Patrick proposed a toast. 'To Moira, the most beautiful woman in New York and Pleasantvale.'

She touched her glass to his. 'To Patrick, the man for all seasons.'

Kit chimed in, 'And to "A World of Difference".'

Smiling at his sister, Patrick added, 'Happiness to all three of us.'

'I'll drink to that,' said Kit fervently.

When the champagne was finished, they went across the road for Chinese food, and well after midnight headed home along the twisting, tree-lined roads, singing tuneless but very enthusiastic medleys of all their favourite songs. The baby sitter was despatched homeward considerably richer than when she had arrived. Kit kissed her brother and Moira good night, said simply, 'I'm very happy for both of you,' and went off to bed, leaving the two of them in the hallway.

'Well,' said Patrick inadequately, 'if this were a play, I should now sweep you into my arms, carry you into the bedroom, and the curtain would go down.'

'However, being real life, you will take yourself and your crutches to your celibate bed.'

'Hell of a bad script.'

'It could be rewritten . . .'

'When Kit leaves, it will be.'

His eyes were wandering over her body in its simple wool skirt and sweater; she felt desire leap to agonising, aching life and whispered, 'Oh God, Patrick, don't . . .'

Rough-voiced, he said, 'I swear I'll always do my best to make you happy.'

'As will I.'

It was, they both knew, the moment of commitment, more so than the proposal in the bar. Patrick took her hands in his and rested his lips in her palm in a gesture of homage that brought tears to her eyes. Then, separately, each went to bed.

Kit stayed for another week, nor did Moira begrudge her the time, for the Kit who was leaving Pleasantvale was a very different person from the pale, thin-faced woman who had greeted Moira at the airport. The weather had turned unseasonably warm, so Kit had natural colour in her face; she had put on five pounds; and there was a new lightness to her step. She mentioned Sandy's name far more naturally in conversation, she was talking about social contacts she would renew back home and courses she might take; she was more patient with the boys. 'A new woman,' as she said to Moira. 'You made a world of difference!'

They were to leave at noon for the airport. But when Patrick went out to start the Toyota, he discovered that the battery was dead; Kit, the last person to use the vehicle, had left the headlights on. 'Oh, Pat, I'm sorry,' Kit wailed. 'It was foggy early this morning when I went to the store, that's why I turned them on . . . what'll we do?'

'Call Dave, I guess, and see if we can borrow the truck. You'll arrive at the airport in style, Sis.'

'Will we all fit in the truck?'

'No, we won't, dammit. Moira, either you or I will have to drive Kit in—we can't both go.'

'You go,' Moira said promptly, knowing how strong the bond was between Kit and Patrick and not wanting to deprive them of a last chance to chat. 'Your ankle's okay now, isn't it?'

'Yeah . . . I'd better phone Dave.'

Patrick disappeared into the house. 'How dumb can you get,' Kit groaned, hoisting Daniel higher on her hip. 'Sorry, Moira.'

'That's all right, I'll lie out in the sun for a while. Kit, I'm so glad we've got to know each other, and I know we'll see each other again soon.'

'I expect to be invited to the wedding,' Kit said impishly. 'So does Peter.'

'You both shall be.'

Kit looked around with a sigh of regret. 'I almost envy you being able to stay here—it's so beautiful.'

Snow still huddled in the hollows, blindingly bright, but in the valley the stream bubbled seaward, released from its winter coat of ice. The hills waited patiently for yet another summer; the crows mocked the world from among the spruce trees.

Then Patrick came back out. 'Dave's on his way up. He'll tow the Toyota back to his place and recharge the battery while we're gone. I can pick it up on the way home. Sure you've got everything, Kit?'

'I've got Peter, Daniel, and the suitcases. Peter's got his truck and Daniel's got his teddy bear. The plane would have to turn around if we forgot the teddy bear. So I guess I've got the essentials. If I've left anything else behind, it means I'll be back. For the wedding,' she added meaningfully. 'No sneaking off to the registry office, Patrick Casey.'

'Whose wedding is it?' her brother demanded.

She grinned. 'As the groom, you're just the excuse for a good party.'

'I resent that! Do you——'

'Here's Dave,' said Moira loudly.

'*You* don't think I'm only an excuse for a party, do you, Moira?'

A party wasn't what I had in mind. She blushed, said lamely, 'Oh, no,' and blushed again as she realised he was reading her mind.

As Dave's truck roared up the driveway Patrick said for her ears alone, 'A party for two would be all right.'

'Three o'clock this afternoon?' she murmured.

'It's a date.'

Dave had backed the truck around so he could hitch the Toyota to a towing chain. Peter watched, fascinated, asking a series of questions which Dave answered as thoroughly as if Peter were a customer at a garage. Patrick gave Moira a quick kiss. 'Back as soon as I can.'

'Drive carefully.' She watched him get in the Toyota; his limp was virtually gone. Then she went over to help Kit. Daniel gave her a wet, gurgling kiss; Peter put his thin little arms around her neck in a hug that almost choked her; Kit kissed her, tears in her eyes. ''Bye, Moira—thanks for everything. You did wonders for my morale.'

'And you gave me the idea for a new career. I'll keep you posted on any developments. Take care of yourself, Kit—and all the best.' Platitudinous words, but she meant them from her heart.

Peter climbed in the truck, his mother followed, and Moira handed Daniel over, complete with the all-important teddy bear. Dave put the truck in gear. The chain pulled taut and the two vehicles rolled down the driveway. Moira stood waving until they were out of sight. Then she went back into the house.

She spent an hour tidying and vacuuming, finding one of Peter's Dinky toys under the chesterfield and a pair of Daniel's socks in with her own laundry. She organised a meal for the evening. She had a leisurely bath. And still there was an hour left before she could reasonably expect Patrick home.

On the southern side of the house Patrick had built a verandah with an enclosed alcove, perfect for sun-bathing, for it trapped the heat yet was sheltered from the wind; she and Kit had spent a fair amount of time there the last few days. She hauled out a foam mattress

covered with flowered cotton, and took off her outer
clothes; when she had packed for this trip, she had not
included a bikini, so she had been sunning herself in her
underwear, as had Kit: Patrick had been warned to stay
in the study. Now he would not have to do so, for they
would be alone, she thought, stretching out on the
mattress. No Kit, no Peter or Daniel. Only the two of
them. Would he kiss her? Would he touch her body as
he had that night in his big bed? And would they catch
fire from each other, as they had then? She felt a shiver
ripple along her spine, and knew she was afraid.

The sun was hot, hotter than yesterday. It would not
do for her to tan with strap marks on her shoulders;
Derek would be displeased. She undid her bra and
slipped out of it, then impulsively stripped off her bikini
briefs, knowing she would hear Patrick's return in time
to put them back on again. She did not think she
wanted him to find her naked. She lay for a while on
her back, then rolled over on her stomach. The crows
were arguing among themselves, muttering like old
women who see too much of each other. The wind
sighed in the tree tops. The sun was deliciously warm,
soothing the tension from her body, bathing her in
peace. Her eyes closed.

Moira did not hear the rattle of stones or the purr of
the motor as the Toyota came up the driveway. She did
not hear the man's footsteps in the house, nor his voice
calling her name. She did not see him step outside and
discover the long, lissom body stretched out on the
mattress, face hidden in a cloud of tawny hair. She did
not see him slowly start to remove his own clothes, until
he stood there naked, body outlined by the sun, his
shadow falling across her back.

But she did feel him. From the depths of a sun-
drenched sleep she felt her spine being stroked, slowly
and rhythmically, from her shoulders to her hips. Over
and over again, a warm and repetitive touch that
brought her back to reality. She lay still, knowing it was
Patrick, and willing now that the moment had come to

give herself up to him. His thighs were clasping her hips; his hands moved to the curve of her waist and the gentle swell of her breasts.

She pushed back her hair and very slowly rolled over. He was straddling her, his naked body limned by the sun, powerful and ready for her. She felt no fear, only wonder and pride and a surge of longing. She took his hands in hers and drew him down to her.

His kiss set the tone for their lovemaking, for it was as slow and subtle as if they had all the time in the world. His mouth moved to drift across her cheekbones and close her lids, while his fingers moulded the softness of her breasts. She savoured each sensation, content to let him have the lead, feeling the sweet, aching tension sing along her nerves, gathering in intensity as his lips encircled her nipples and his knees edged her thighs open. Her eyes were still closed. Through her fingertips she traced the smooth planes of his back, warmed by the sun, and the broad arc of his ribcage, thrilling to the heavy beat of his heart, wanting this languorous, infinitely sensual exploration to last forever.

'Look at me,' Patrick said huskily.

His face was intent, deeply serious; his eyes burned like the blue of the sky behind him. She smiled up at him with such complete trust that his features constricted. Seizing her hand, he brought it to his mouth, bowing his head over it. 'I don't want to hurt you.'

'You won't,' she said gently. That it should be he who was afraid banished any fear she might have felt. With a touching awkwardness that betrayed her inexperience she moved her hips under his, saw him shudder with pleasure, and more confidently moved again. His hands slid downward as they had done once before, and again her body's response was so all-encompassing that involuntarily she cried out. With all the control and sensitivity that he was capable of he brought her, trembling and whimpering, to the very edge of need before he entered her. She was beyond fear

or pain. She arched her back to gather him in, her body
writhing, her hair tossed on the mattress, and his
desperate, anguished cry mingled with her own. The
dam broke. The waters tumbled free and flung them to
the shore.

Only gradually did Moira become aware that she was
crying, clutching at Patrick as if she would never let him
go. He had fallen across her; his heartbeat mingled with
her own, his back was slippery with sweat, he was very
heavy. She said wonderingly, 'Patrick, Patrick . . . is it
always like that? I had no idea . . . oh Patrick, I love
you so much.'

He kissed the trail of tears from her cheek. 'Did I
hurt you?'

She managed the faintest of smiles, although her lips
had a tendency to quiver. 'If you did, I was in no state
to notice.' How could she put into words what his
possession of her had been like? 'I feel as though I've
died and been reborn,' she whispered. 'For the first time
in my life I understand why I'm made the way I am . . .
to take you in, be filled with you.'

'To become as one flesh.'

'The old words are often the best, aren't they?'

'You will marry me, darling Moira?'

'Yes.'

'As soon as possible?'

'Yes.'

His laugh was triumphant, from deep in his chest.
Grabbing her hands, he pulled her to her feet. 'Come
with me.'

Running a little to keep up with him, she followed
him to the front of the house where the valley was
spread before them. 'Someone will see us,' she gasped.

'There's no one to see us.' And indeed the fields were
deserted, the trees and incurious sky their only
witnesses. Patrick cupped his hands around his mouth
and yelled, 'I love Moira.' The hills flung his words
back. 'Love . . . ove . . . Moira . . . ra . . . ra.'

She threw back her head and laughed, a peal of pure

joy, and the hills laughed back. 'I love Patrick,' she shouted. His name bounced back across the valley. 'Rick . . . rick . . . rick.' She laughed again, as carefree and happy as a young girl, saw Patrick's eyes darken, and knew before he picked her up what was going to happen. 'Where are we going?' she murmured, nibbling at his chest.

'To bed.'

'A man of few words.'

'All good dramatists should know that at times actions speak louder than words.' He had pushed open the kitchen door and was carrying her down the hall.

She tickled him in a very suggestive place. 'What sort of actions?' she said innocently.

He put her down by the bed, the smile fading from his face. 'Make love to me, Moira,' he said hoarsely. 'Show me how much you love me.'

She was bolder now, more sure of herself, no longer the inexperienced virgin. She kissed him and stroked him and touched him, learning what pleased him, what made the breath rasp in his throat and the blood pound in his veins, until she had brought him to a pitch of longing that he could no longer bear. He took her fiercely, and fiercely she welcomed him, and the ancient rhythms conquered them both.

They slept for a while, naked and exhausted in each other's arms. And when they woke, as if there had been no break in the conversation, Patrick said, 'How soon will you marry me?'

'I won't run away, you know.' Moira was lying on her side, facing him, their heads together on the pillow. Smiling, she added, 'At the moment I'm not sure I can walk, let alone run.'

'I'm too much for you, am I? Moira, I want the whole world—not just the hills of Pleasantvale—to know we belong to each other.'

She kissed his ear. 'We have to give Kit enough time to get home, unpack, do a wash, and then pack again.'

'That's true.'

'And you have to go to Scots Bay with me to meet my parents. Da is of the old-fashioned school. You'll be required to ask for my hand in marriage, and you'll have to assure him that writing plays is a perfectly respectable occupation—that pays. Real money.'

He chuckled. 'Will Archie be lying in wait for me?'

'I hope not. I hope by now Archie will be dating Lorraine.'

'I can see this isn't going to be simple.'

She said, suddenly serious, 'Patrick, did you mean what you said about moving to the shore if I were to start my business in Halifax?'

'Yes, I meant it.'

'But you love it here so much. Won't you resent having to leave?'

'I won't sell the place, Moira. I'll probably never do that. But I'd like to live by the ocean—I'm not martyring myself. And it's important to me for you to be happy.'

'Will "A World of Difference" work out, do you think?'

'It's got very good possibilities. You'll have to do market research, check everything out with business people, accountants, the like, maybe start small and work up. Initially you'll have to work very hard, I'm sure.'

'I'm not afraid of work. I'm glad you understand that I need something of my own.'

'I couldn't live without writing. Why should I expect you to be different?'

'If you're locked up in the study trying to start the first act and I'm tearing around Halifax trying to run a business ... will we have time for each other? We mustn't neglect our marriage.' Her voice was passionate with conviction, for she had just discovered the truth of her own words. 'That comes first.'

'As long as we both know that, we'll be all right. And if we're in danger of forgetting, I'll haul you off to bed to remind you.'

'Or *I'll* haul *you*,' she said saucily. 'A little more difficult in view of the disparity in size, but I'm sure I could manage.'

'You'll never have to depend on brute strength to get me into bed with you, darling. Just do this. Or this.'

'Oh, really?' She batted her lashes, acutely aware of him guiding her hand down his body. 'I never would have guessed.'

'Believe me, if I'm all caught up in the first act and you do that to me, it'll make a world of difference.'

'I'll have to remember that.' She repeated obediently, 'A world of difference, hmm?'

Mills & Boon

Take 4
Exciting Books
Absolutely
FREE

Love, romance, intrigue... all are captured for you by Mills & Boon's top-selling authors. By becoming a regular reader of Mills & Boon's Romances you can enjoy 6 superb new titles every month plus a whole range of special benefits: your very own personal membership card, a free monthly newsletter packed with recipes, competitions, exclusive book offers and a monthly guide to the stars, plus extra bargain offers and big cash savings.

AND an Introductory FREE GIFT for YOU.
Turn over the page for details.

The perfect holiday romance.

ACT OF BETRAYAL Sara Craven	**YOU OWE ME** Penny Jordan
MAN HUNT Charlotte Lamb	**LOVERS IN THE AFTERNOON** Carole Mortimer

Have a more romantic holiday this summer with the Mills & Boon holiday pack.

Four brand new titles, attractively packaged for only £4.40.

The holiday pack is published on the 14th June. Look out for it where you buy Mills & Boon.

The Rose of Romance

New from Violet Winspear, one of Mills and Boon's best-selling authors, a longer romance of mystery, intrigue, suspense and love. Almost twice the length of a standard romance for just £1.95. Published on the 14th of June.

The Rose of Romance

A romance of searing passion set amid the barbaric
splendour of Richard the Lionheart's Crusade. Intrigue
turns to love across the battlefield... a longer historical
novel from Mills and Boon, for only £2.25.
Published on 12th of July.

The Rose of Romance

ROMANCE

Next month's romances from Mills & Boon

Each month, you can choose from a world of variety in romance with Mills & Boon. These are the new titles to look out for next month.

MERRINGANNEE BLUFF Kerry Allyne
IMPETUOUS MARRIAGE Rosemary Carter
FANTASY Emma Darcy
THE TROUBLE WITH BRIDGES Emma Goldrick
WHO'S BEEN SLEEPING IN MY BED? C. Lamb
COME NEXT SUMMER Leigh Michaels
RETURN TO ARKADY Jeneth Murrey
AT THE END OF THE DAY Betty Neels
A PROMISE TO DISHONOUR Jessica Steele
EXECUTIVE LADY Sophie Weston

Buy them from your usual paperback stockist, or write to: Mills & Boon Reader Service, P.O. Box 236, Thornton Rd, Croydon, Surrey CR9 3RU, England. Readers in South Africa-write to: Mills & Boon Reader Service of Southern Africa, Private Bag X3010, Randburg, 2125.

Mills & Boon
the rose of romance